THE UNPUBLISHED SPIKE MILLIGAN

BOX 18

Also published by Fourth Estate:

The Essential Spike Milligan
edited by Alexander Games

The Compulsive Spike Milligan
edited by Norma Farnes

Spike: An Intimate Memoir
by Norma Farnes

THE UNPUBLISHED SPIKE MILLIGAN

BOX 18

Edited by
Norma Farnes

FOURTH ESTATE • London

This edition produced for The Book People Ltd.,
Hall Wood Avenue, Haydock, St Helens, WA11 9UL

First published in Great Britain in 2006 by Fourth Estate

An imprint of HarperCollinsPublishers
77–85 Fulham Palace Road
London W6 8JB
www.4thestate.co.uk

1 3 5 7 9 10 8 6 4 2

A catalogue record for this book is available from the British Library
ISBN: 0-00-777973-9

Typeset and designed by Estuary English

Printed and bound in Slovenia by MKTPrint

This book is for my mentor and friend
Lawrence Drizen

ACKNOWLEDGMENTS

I would like to thank Janet Spearman for her help not just with this book but over the years; Louise Haines, my editor, who always has faith in me; Alan ('Groucho') Matthews, a true Milligan fan; Eric Sykes, for always being there; Joan Taylor, my mother's angel; Pamela Lester, for all her support over the years; and for just being him, Bill Kenwright.

Special thanks to Jack Clarke for his encouragement, support and love.

EDITOR'S NOTE

I have called this book *The Unpublished Spike Milligan*, and that's what it is. If anything has slipped through the net and has been published before, *mea culpa* – but please, please: no letters of complaint saying you've seen it before. I did my best. If the old sod were here he'd say, 'That's what worries me.'

CONTENTS

Fame at last.

INTRODUCTION

Spike's list of files (Box 14).

BOX 18 – IDEAS. An extraordinary title, but then Spike was an extraordinary man. His public persona was that of a manic, scatty, undisciplined character, someone who spoke with machine-gun delivery, a thoroughly disorganised individual. This was the complete opposite of Spike in the office; he was the most focused person I have ever met: disciplined, methodical and meticulous about his filing system. Yes – his filing system: large box files for his office work, fourteen and a half inches by ten and a half, numbered 1, 2, 3, 4, etc. Then his household files were ten inches by seven and a half inches, marked a, b, c, d, etc. The labels on the files were in his own calligraphy handwriting, describing what they contained, all except Box 1, which quite simply bore the title 'Files'. This contained one piece of paper listing all the box files and their contents. For example:

Box 18 – Ideas. This contained Spike's ideas. He would scribble a poem and put it in this file. Sometimes it would be incomplete and he would work on it, perhaps a week or a month later, or it would be 'chucked'. The file contained ideas for speeches, stories or sketches for one of his television programmes. Sometimes we would sit and go through them together – and, of course, he would occasionally say, 'I'll bin that. I didn't realise I could be that unfunny.' The longest 'idea' was a children's story called 'The Magic Staircase'. It was in the file for about three years. He would take it out, look at it, put it back and say, 'I like this. It's a good idea. I'll keep it.' One day he took it out of the file and said, 'Today's the day for "The Magic Staircase".' He worked on it for two weeks, by which time it was a novel mixing fact and fiction. It was published in 1990 under the title *It Ends With Magic* and is, in my opinion, Spike's most skilled piece of writing.

One thing never ceased to amaze me: when he decided to work on any one of his ideas he would sit at the typewriter and the writing simply flowed. He really was blessed with a natural gift. Now, having explained Spike's meticulous filing system, every now and then the other Spike would emerge. He'd have a tantrum and want something from one of his files NOW. He would take out whatever he needed and, when he had finished with it, throw it in the bin. So the next time he needed it and it wasn't there, someone had 'fucked up my filing system'. Or, when he was manic, he would for no apparent reason decide to rearrange two or three of the files, or to amalgamate them. He'd stick pieces of paper over the existing meticulous piece of paper, in some cases covering up the list of contents. That's when the trouble would start – and, believe me, this was not infrequent. When the storm was over he would sit quietly and start all over again; it was ever so.

The idea for this book came to me when I was looking for a story that Spike had written. He called it a 'life after death story'. It was a particular favourite of mine and I thought his writing had really captured the essence of life after death. It had been an idea for a radio programme and I had wanted to include it, together with some other stories, in a book entitled *Short Stories by Spike Milligan.* I thought it was too good to lay fallow in Box 18. But, as always, other ideas captured Spike's imagination and it would be, 'Promise, Norm – next time.' Then he eventually did write another story – 'The Bing Bong Circus' – and I foolishly thought we were on the way, yet again. Not to be: 'Bing Bong' was added to Box 18.

My favourite of all the children's books was *Badjelly the Witch*, and I tried to persuade him on several occasions to write a follow-up. Again, it was started and added to – and ended up you know where. Trying to persuade Spike to do something when he wasn't in the mood was like 'swimming in porridge' (one of his expressions). So, to encourage him, I asked him to draw a Badjelly, a dragon and a castle. He did. Progress! He sent it to me and it wasn't one of his best efforts, either in order to shut me up or a case of 'That's the best I can do and that's that.' I sent it back to him with a note saying, '6/10. Could do better. Talk to me.' He did. He sent it back and, sure enough, it had indeed been one of the occasions on which 'That's the best I can do and that's that.' So why wasn't it thrown away? Kismet. You know what? I've become so fond of that drawing that it makes me smile every time I see it, so I've included it in this book.

While I was in the middle of smiling and reflecting on that incident, I recalled some of the quirky drawings he had done for his poetry books. I looked through them – nostalgia, I suppose – and that's when I realised that they'd make great greetings cards. I approached my favourite card company, Woodmansterne, who were enthusiastic and have since printed a selection of his drawings – though not, of course, the badly drawn dragon, which was returned to the Ideas file.

And it was then that I wondered: would a publisher be interested in a volume of unpublished works by Spike? Louise Haines, Spike's editor, was enthusiastic. I had only intended to publish the Ideas file, but I then recalled all the letters he had written. In my opinion, those I have included show the various facets of Spike's personality, a personality inherited from his mother. I told Spike that if I had a vision of one woman who had built the British Empire, it was his mother. Like her son she was an avid letter writer and wrote to me almost every week for over twenty years. So, to give an insight into her character, I've included just one of her letters. She would have liked that.

Some years ago, when I started to write *Spike: An Intimate Memoir*, Spike gave me his diaries – 'to help you, because you are no bloody good at keeping diaries, so if I give you mine it will keep you off my back. Otherwise it will be, "Do you remember this, Spike?" or "When did we do that, Spike?"' So I've also included some pages from his diaries that I hope will show what a complex and captivating man he was, and give you some idea of his energy and the multitude of activities he could and did embrace in any one day.

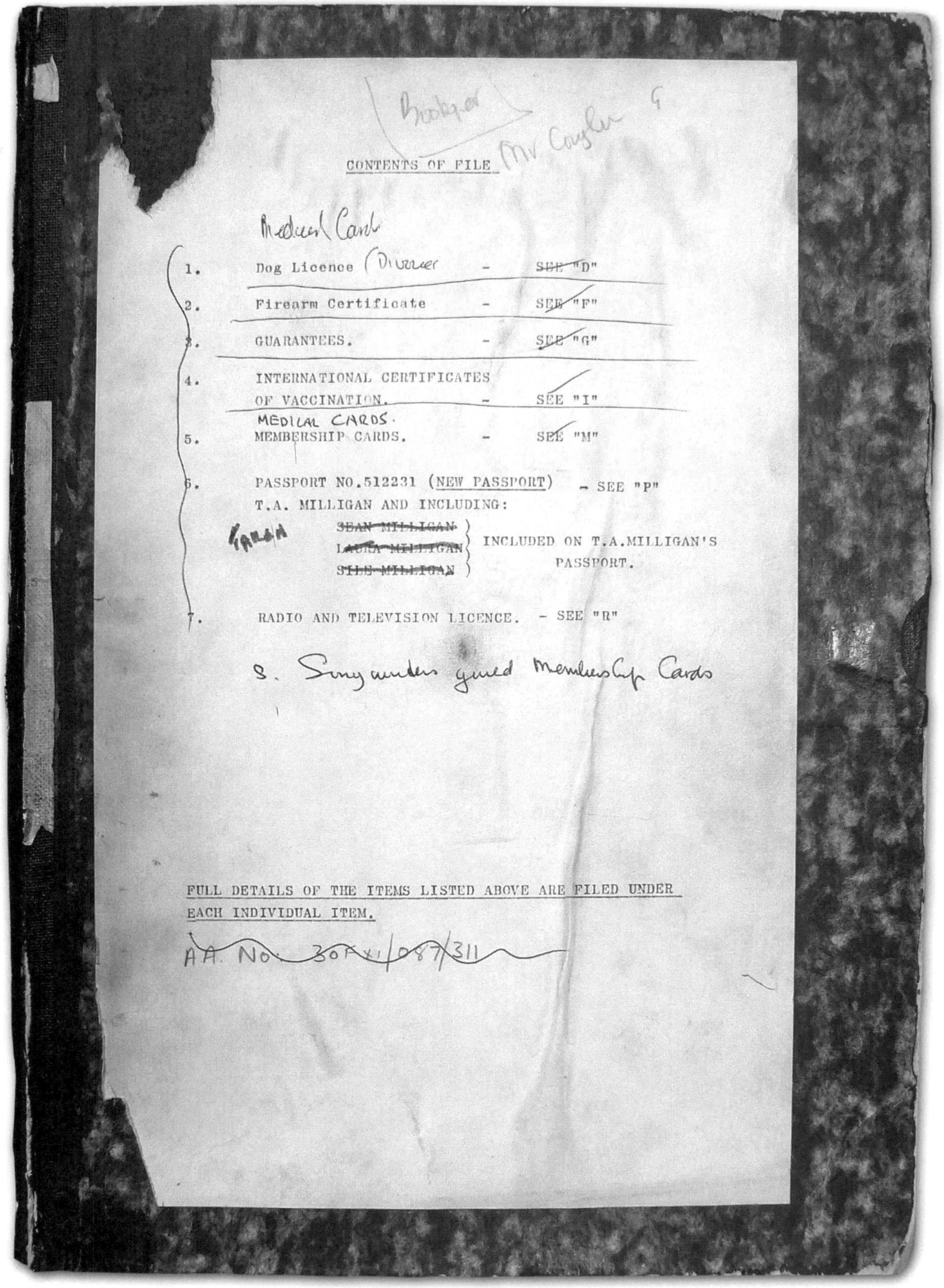

CONTENTS OF FILE Mr Cougher

Medical Card

1. Dog Licence (Diviner - ~~SEE~~ "D"
2. Firearm Certificate - ~~SEE~~ "F"
3. GUARANTEES. - ~~SEE~~ "G"
4. INTERNATIONAL CERTIFICATES OF VACCINATION. - SEE "I"
5. MEDICAL CARDS. MEMBERSHIP CARDS. - SEE "M"
6. PASSPORT NO.512231 (NEW PASSPORT) - SEE "P"
T.A. MILLIGAN AND INCLUDING:
~~SEAN MILLIGAN~~
~~LAURA MILLIGAN~~
~~SILE MILLIGAN~~
INCLUDED ON T.A.MILLIGAN'S PASSPORT.
7. RADIO AND TELEVISION LICENCE. - SEE "R"

8. Sony unders guied Membership Cards

FULL DETAILS OF THE ITEMS LISTED ABOVE ARE FILED UNDER EACH INDIVIDUAL ITEM.

AA. No. 30FX1/087/311

Each file had a detailed list of exactly what was inside.

Some of Spike's files.

MADE IN ENGLAND
TRADES MEN
EAST-LIGHT
Receipts
Stewart Stone Ltd
Laundry
Dry Cleaning.
from 19
to 19
F
WHEN RE-ORDERING THIS FILE SPECIFY
LOCKSPRING-BOX
8vo size
B.E.L.L. Barking & London. LABEL COPYRIGHTED.
MADE IN ENGLAND
EAST-LIGHT
Receipts
PATENT BOX-FILE WITH LOCKSPRING
School fees
" meals
" Travel
from 19
to 19
N
WHEN RE-ORDERING THIS FILE SPECIFY
LOCKSPRING-BOX
8vo size
B.E.L.L. Barking & London. LABEL COPYRIGHTED.
TRADESMEN
EAST-LIGHT
RECEIPTS
PATENT BOX-FILE WITH LOCKSPRING
Car Hire
Garages.
Petrol, Oil, Etc
from 19
to 19
Receipts P
WHEN RE-ORDERING THIS FILE SPECIFY
LOCKSPRING-BOX
8vo size
B.E.L.L. Barking & London. LABEL COPYRIGHTED.

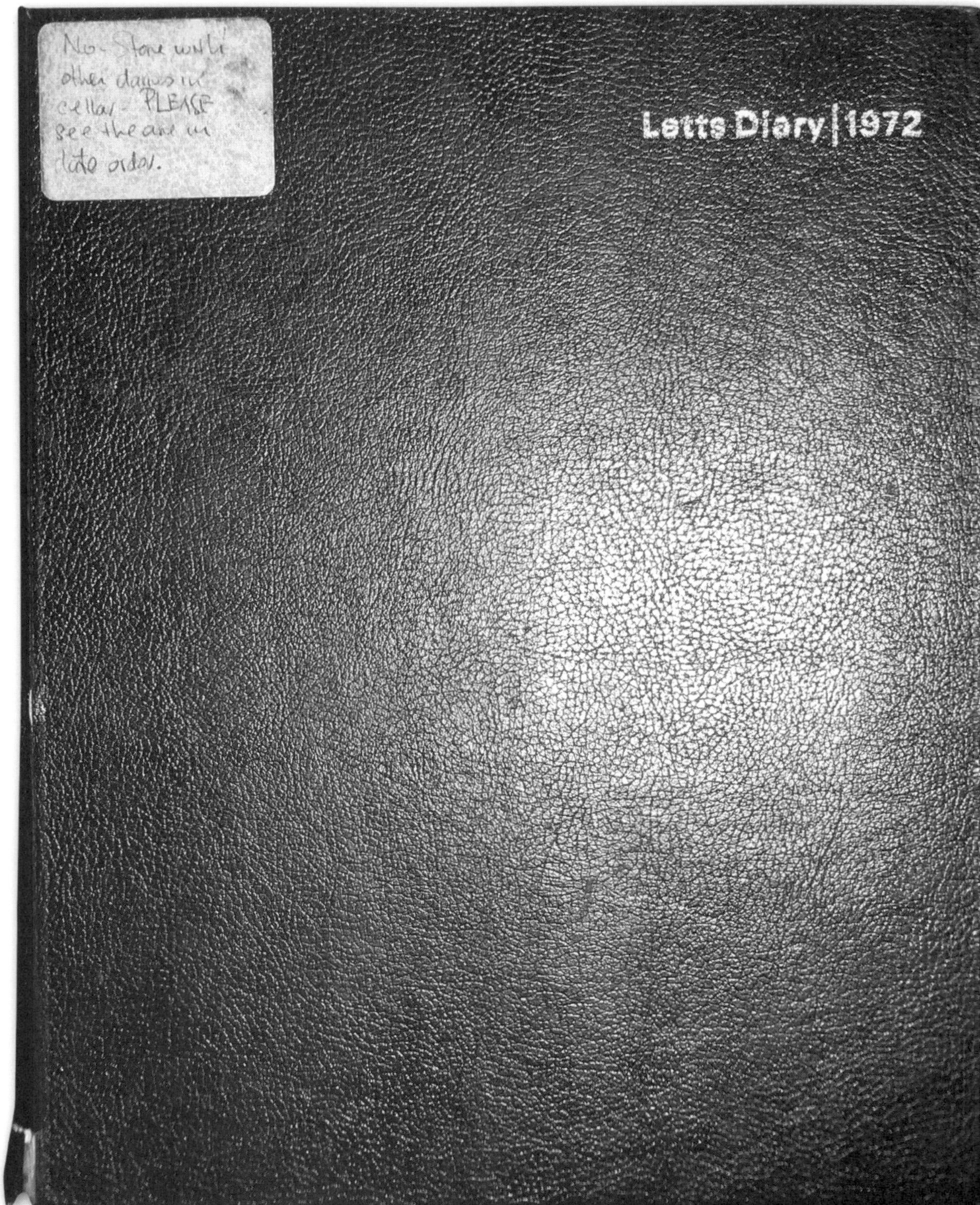

The sticker in the top left corner reads: 'Now store with other diaries in cellar. PLEASE see the(y) are in date order.'

SPIKE'S DIARIES

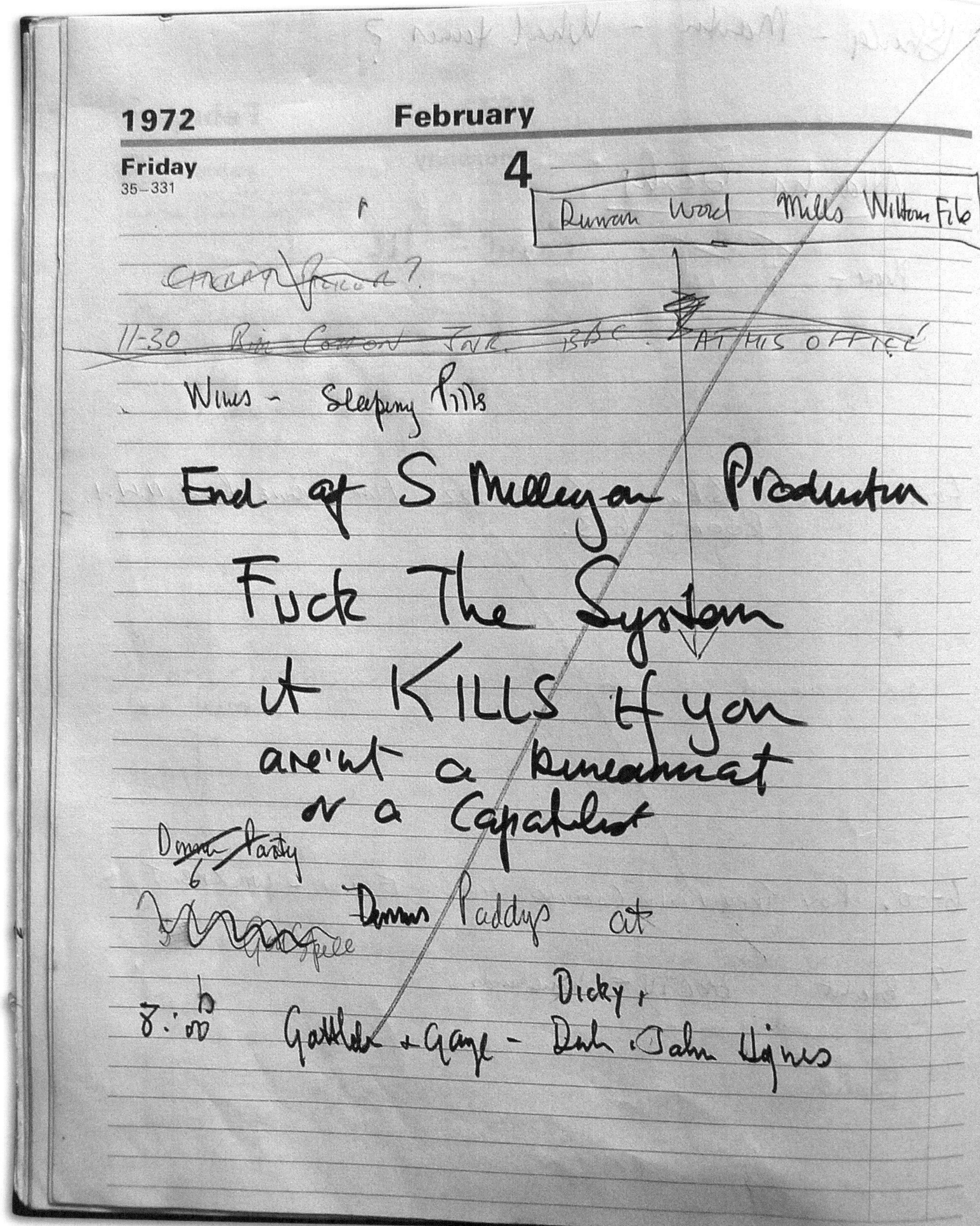

One of the many occasions on which I had obviously told Spike he couldn't have something out of the company. It was the end for him – but not for the company, which is still in existence today.

Sale £5 - 80.

1972 **February**

Saturday **19**
50–316

(1) See Laura give her B&W Drawing out fits.
(2) Hardware - works
(3)

Say 2.00 was 9 Orme
14.30 - 2:30

STEVE WILL PICK YOU UP AT 127 HOLDEN ROAD. ~~11 30 HR~~S.
4-5. PLANE. FLIGHT No. BE 926.
ARRIVE. 5.5 DUBLIN.

5-5. MET AT AIRPORT BY MIKE McWEENY
Hiberman

(P)

IRISH TV. Details later. Tell Paddy. ?
I was told the whole programme was turned over to me to read my book – on arrival I was told this was not so – They would say I was in Dublin to sign – then another author would talk about his book – HANCOCK – Peter 'Measles' Sellers is also on the programme.
Went to airport with Peter Sellers – then Mrs Sellers Bert his Chauffeur – and two TV men

1972 **February**

Monday **21**

52–314 Week 9

SIGN BOOKS IN IRELAND. WHAT SHOP?
WHAT ADDRESS!

12-00 UNTIL 2-00 p.m. SIGN BOOKS.
Easons – O'Connell St nr to Metropole

4-40. LEAVE DUBLIN. FLIGHT NO. BE. 929.
ARRIVE LONDON. 5-40pm.

STEVE WILL PICK YOU UP.
Tell Paddy

(P) Prepare for Hospital
Pyjamas
1 Vest
4 Underpants
Nupercainal? Ask Joe Robson

Packing his bag methodically to go into hospital.

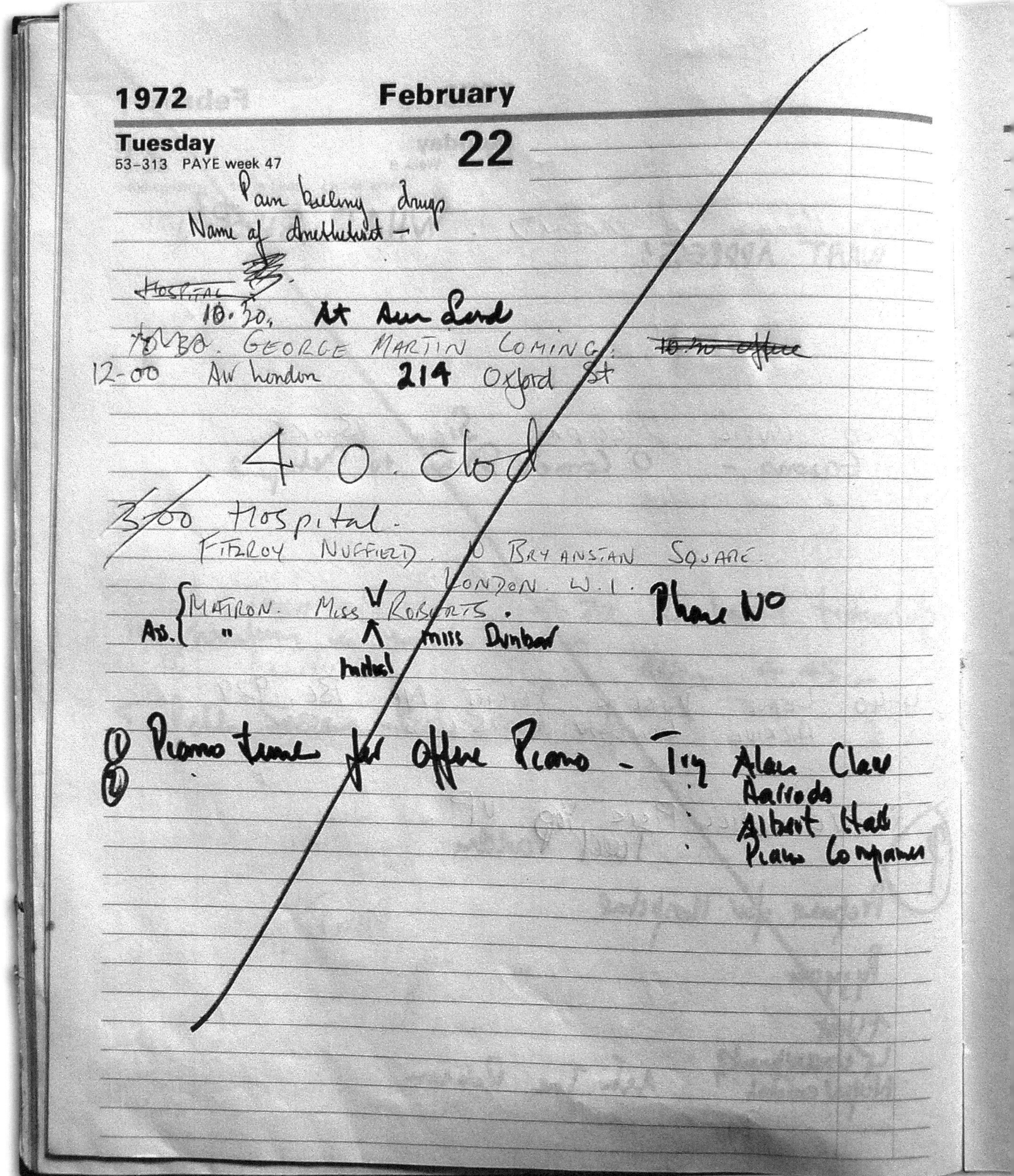

1972 February

Tuesday 22

53–313 PAYE week 47

Pain killing drugs

Name of Anesthetist –

~~HOSPITAL~~

10.30. At Ann Lord

~~10~~ 30. GEORGE MARTIN COMING. ~~10.30 office~~

12-00 Air London 214 Oxford St

4 O. Clock

~~3.00~~ Hospital.

FITZROY NUFFIELD. 10 BRYANSTON SQUARE

LONDON W.1.

MATRON. Miss Roberts. Phone No

Ass. " Miss Dunbar

Initial

(1) Piano tuner for office Piano – Try Alan Clair

(2) Harrods

Albert Hall

Piano Company

Checking the name of the anaesthetist so that he can make sure he is using the right painkillers.

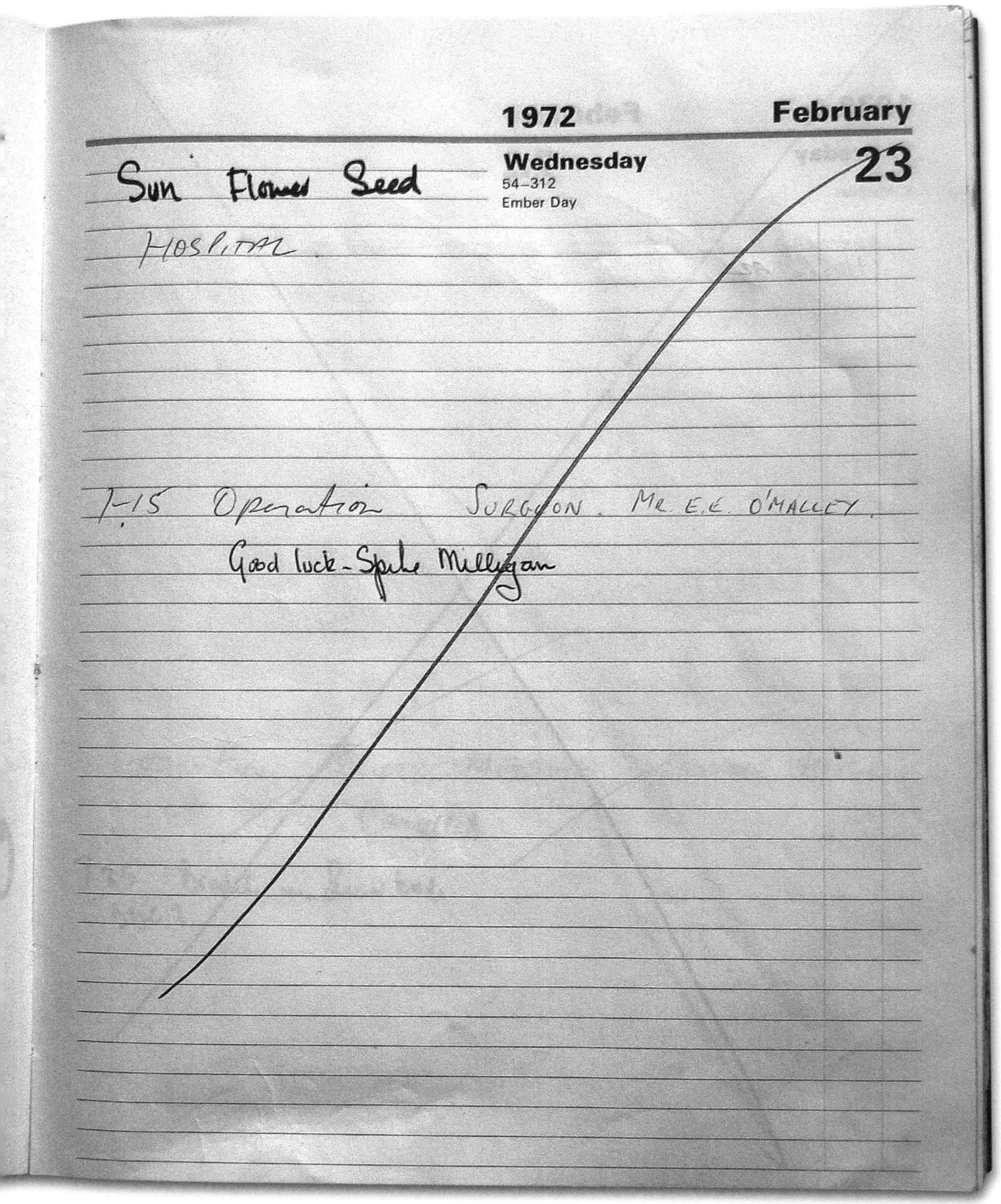

Making sure he has his sunflower seeds and wishing himself good luck – I loved that.

Paddy said she will pick me up before 11 o'clock
She will phone me when shes coming.

1972 **March**

Friday **3**
63–303

Start to write Aquarius

(1) Is Milligan for all Seasons on – write and ask.
(2) What's with Hitler Film?
(3) Go home from hospital – Operation not so bad – I'm glad I overcame my fear of this particular operation – it was one I knew was terribly painful well – it wasn't so bad. Its still very sore and bleeds but I've to see the Doc in a weeks time.

The operation was for haemorrhoids and Spike had been told it would be very painful. He refused any food – hence the sunflower seeds – and Matron Roberts was driven mad by him. He told her he wouldn't eat solids and 'crap broken glass to please you'. He lived on jelly and sunflower seeds instead.

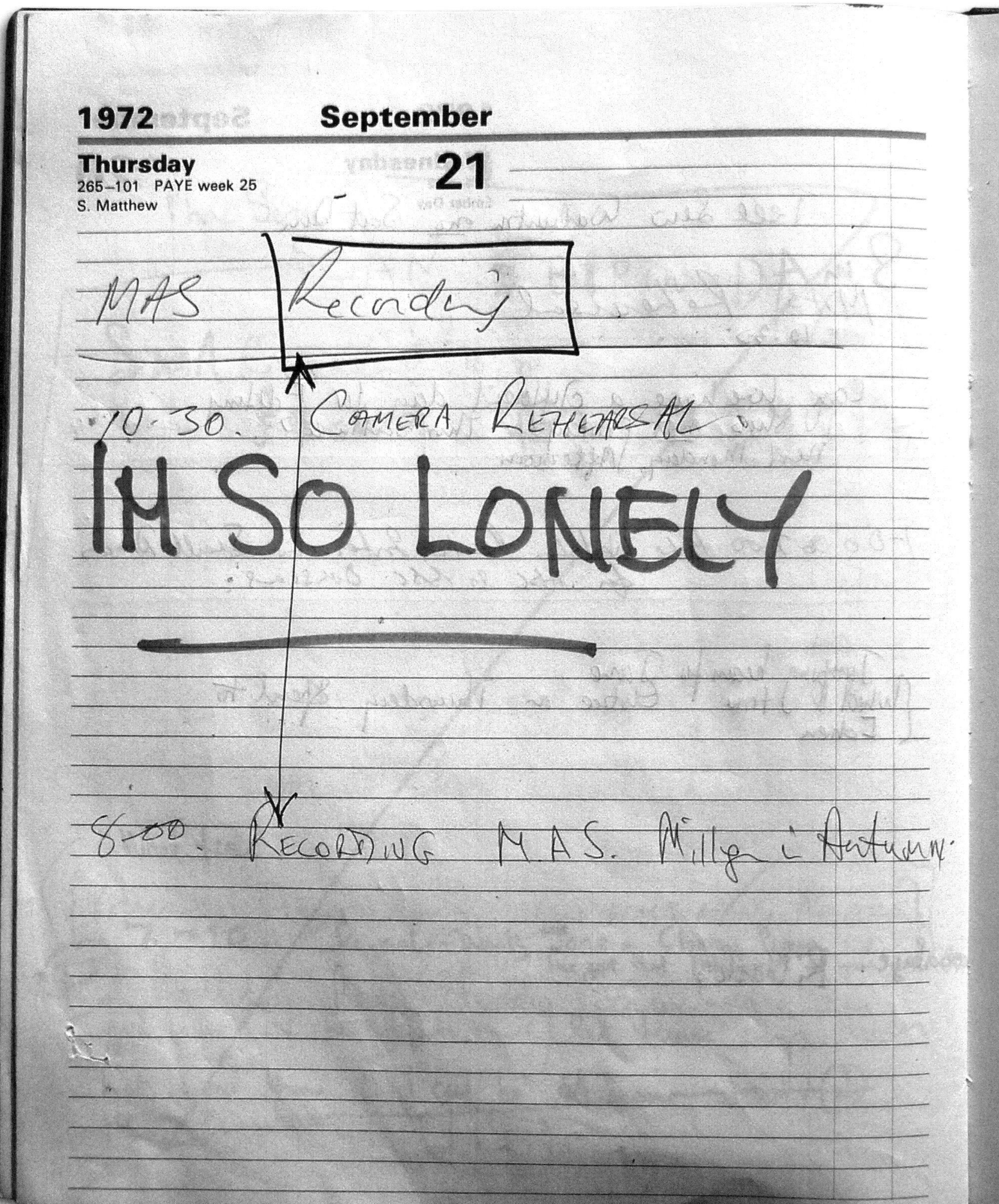
1972 September

Thursday 21

265–101 PAYE week 25

S. Matthew

MAS Recording

10·30. CAMERA REHEARSAL

IM SO LONELY

8·00. RECORDING M.A.S.

This was always the feeling he would get before going into a depression. It never changed.

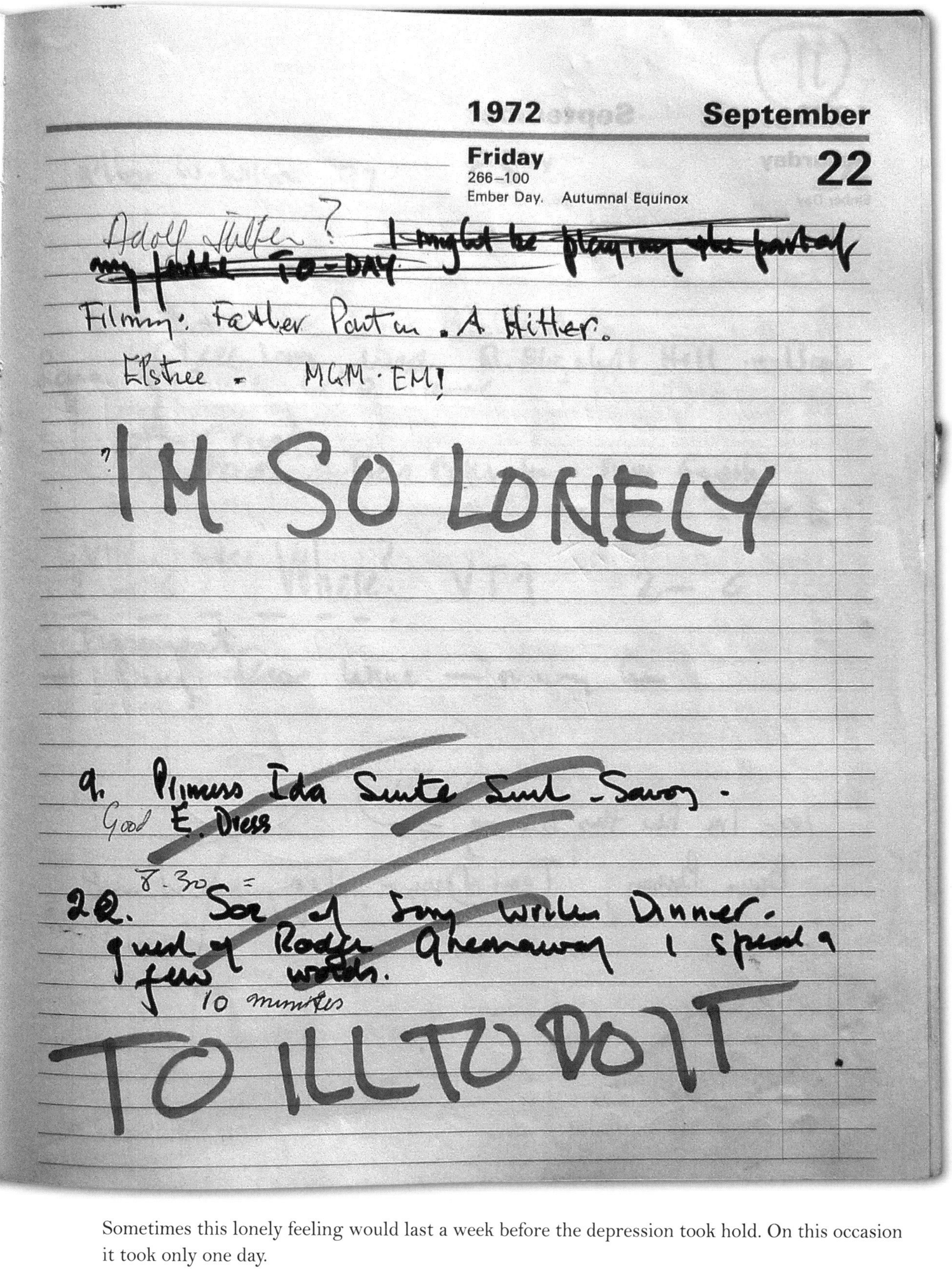
1972 September
Friday 22
266–100
Ember Day. Autumnal Equinox

Adolf Hitler? ~~I might be playing the part of my father TO-DAY.~~

Filming: Father Part in. A Hitler.
Elstree. MGM · EMI

I'M SO LONELY

9. Princess Ida Suite Suit - Savoy.
Good E. Dress

8.30 =
2Q. Soc. of Song Writers Dinner.
guest of Roger Greenaway I speak a few words.
10 minutes

TO ILL TO DO IT.

Sometimes this lonely feeling would last a week before the depression took hold. On this occasion it took only one day.

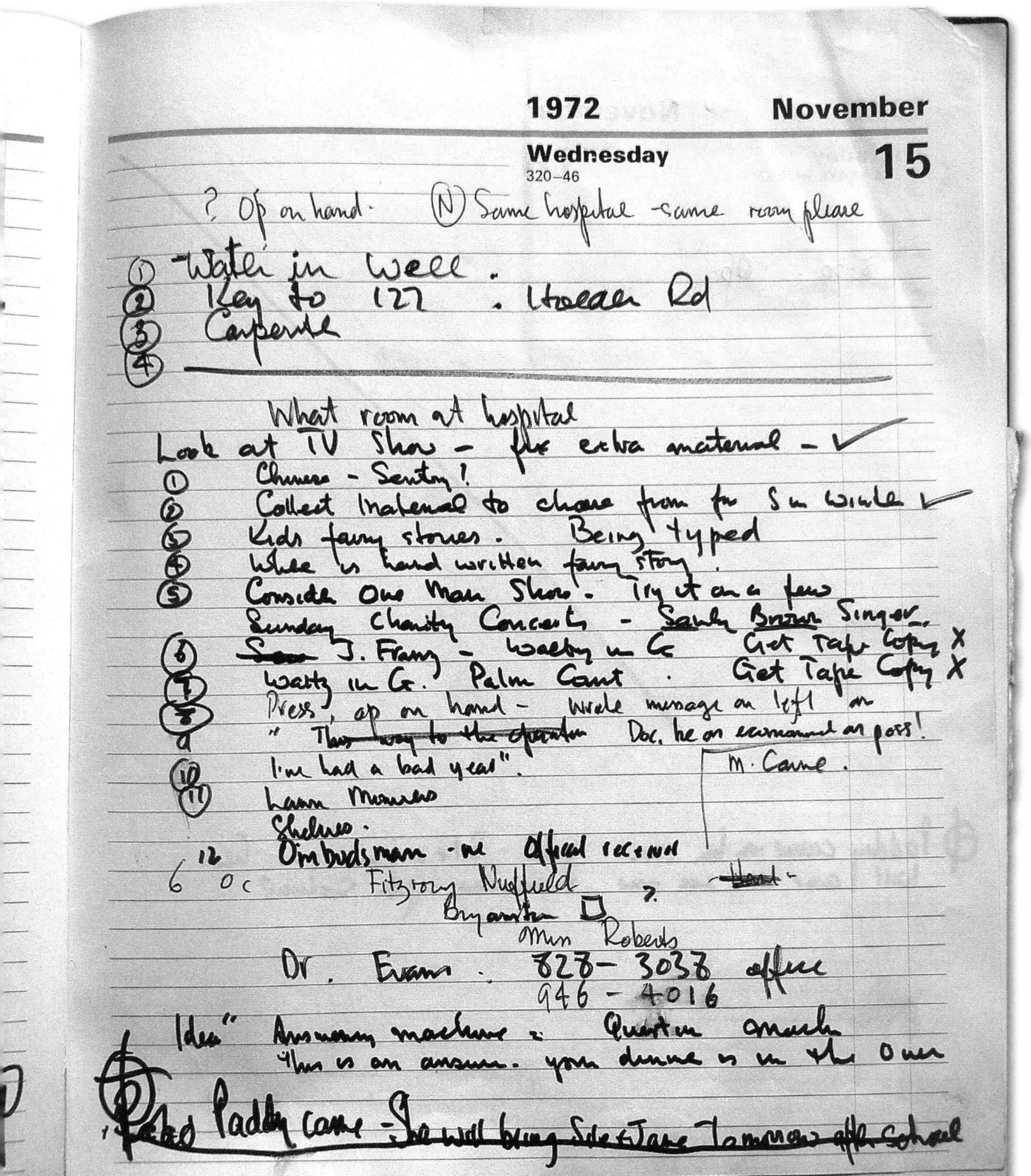

Spike would never admit it but he liked operations. Another one – this time to straighten his finger. Poor Matron Roberts. A list of things to do whilst in hospital.

1972 November

Sunday 19
324–42
25th after Trinity

~~GOOD OLD DAYS B.B.C. LEEDS.~~

· There was a little fly ·

Nov 27

~~In abhorrent memory of Colonel Geo Armstrong Custer US Cavalry who on this day in 1868 · massacred without warning the ~~red~~ village of Chief Black Kettle and his Cheyennes, men - women and children.~~

Mermaid. – Mummings Show

J. Show. — ?

What on earth brought this on?

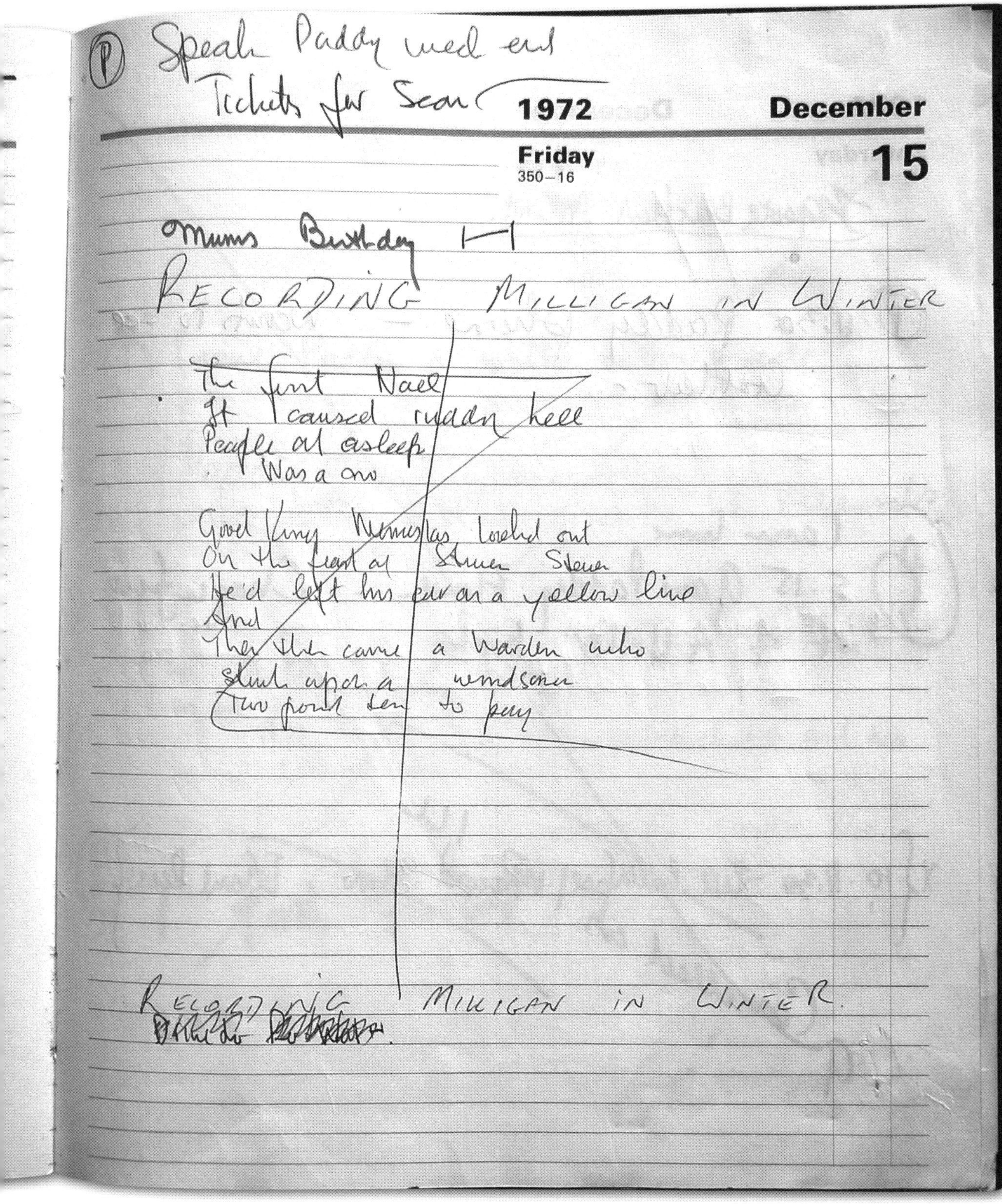

(P) Speak Paddy wed end
Tickets for Sean

1972 December

Friday
350–16

15

Mums Birthday

RECORDING MILLIGAN IN WINTER

~~The first Noel~~
It caused ruddan hell
People all asleep
Was a ono

Good King Wenceslas looked out
On the feast of Stevens Steven
He'd left his car on a yellow line
And
Then there came a Warden who
stuck upon a windscreen
Two pound ten to pay

RECORDING MILLIGAN IN WINTER.

First ideas. He would then either hone them before the show or 'bin them'.

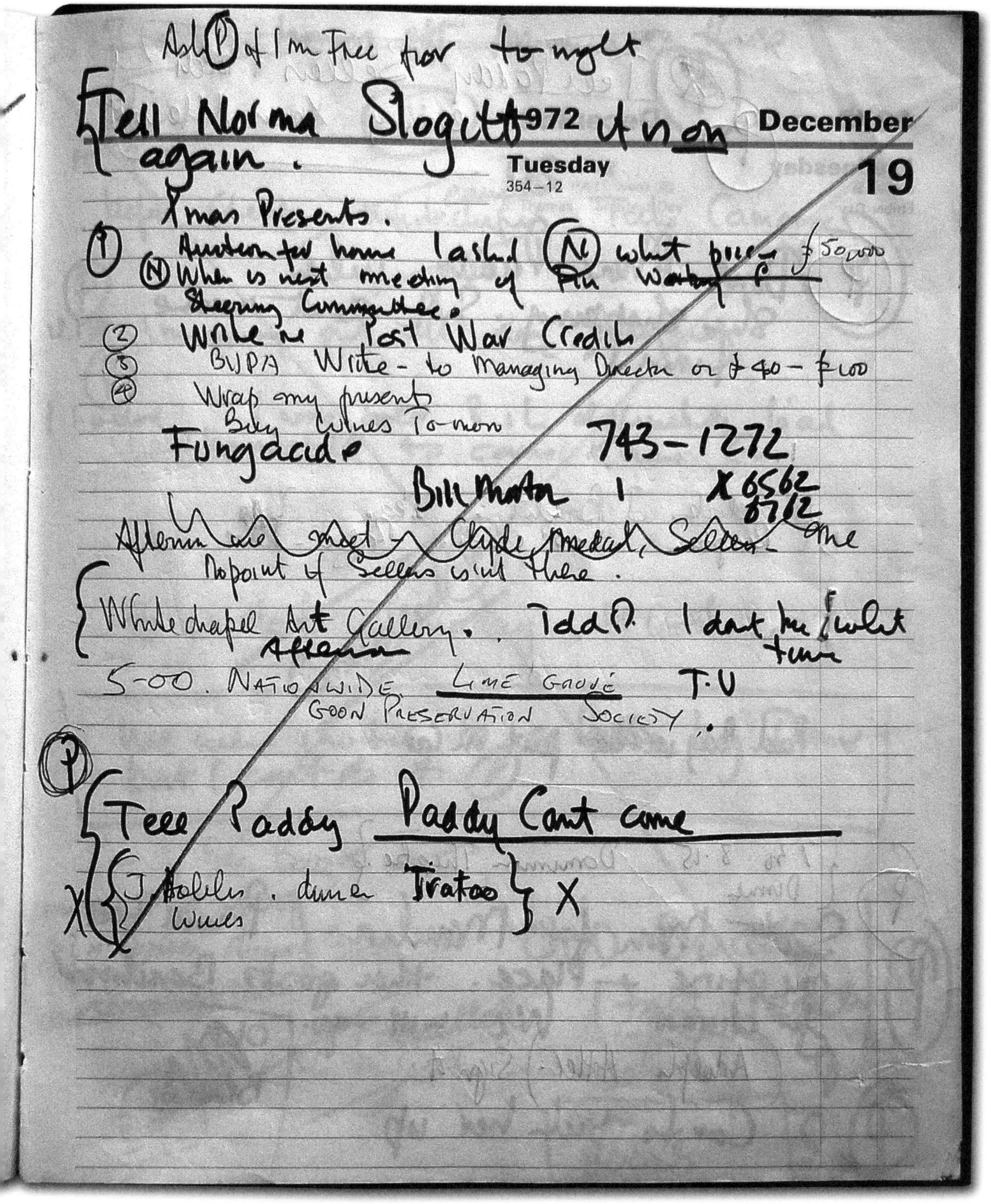

Ask (P) if I'm Free for to-night

Tell Norma Sloggett it is on again.

1972 December

Tuesday

354–12

19

Xmas Presents.

(1) Auction for home I asked (N) what price £50,000

(N) When is next meeting of the Water Steering Committee.

(2) Write re Post War Credits

(3) BUPA Write - to Managing Director or £40 - £100

(4) Wrap my presents

Buy Wines To-morrow

Fungacide 743-1272

Bill Morton 1 X6562 8712

Afternoon [illegible] Clyde, medal, Sellers - me

No point if Sellers isn't there.

Whitechapel Art Gallery. Afternoon. Todd P. I don't know what time

5-00. NATIONWIDE. LIME GROVE T.V

GOON PRESERVATION SOCIETY.

(P) Tell Paddy Paddy Can't come

J. Hobbs . dinner Trattoo X

Wines

Getting himself organised for Christmas. He really did wrap his presents every year. Mind you, he had to remind himself.

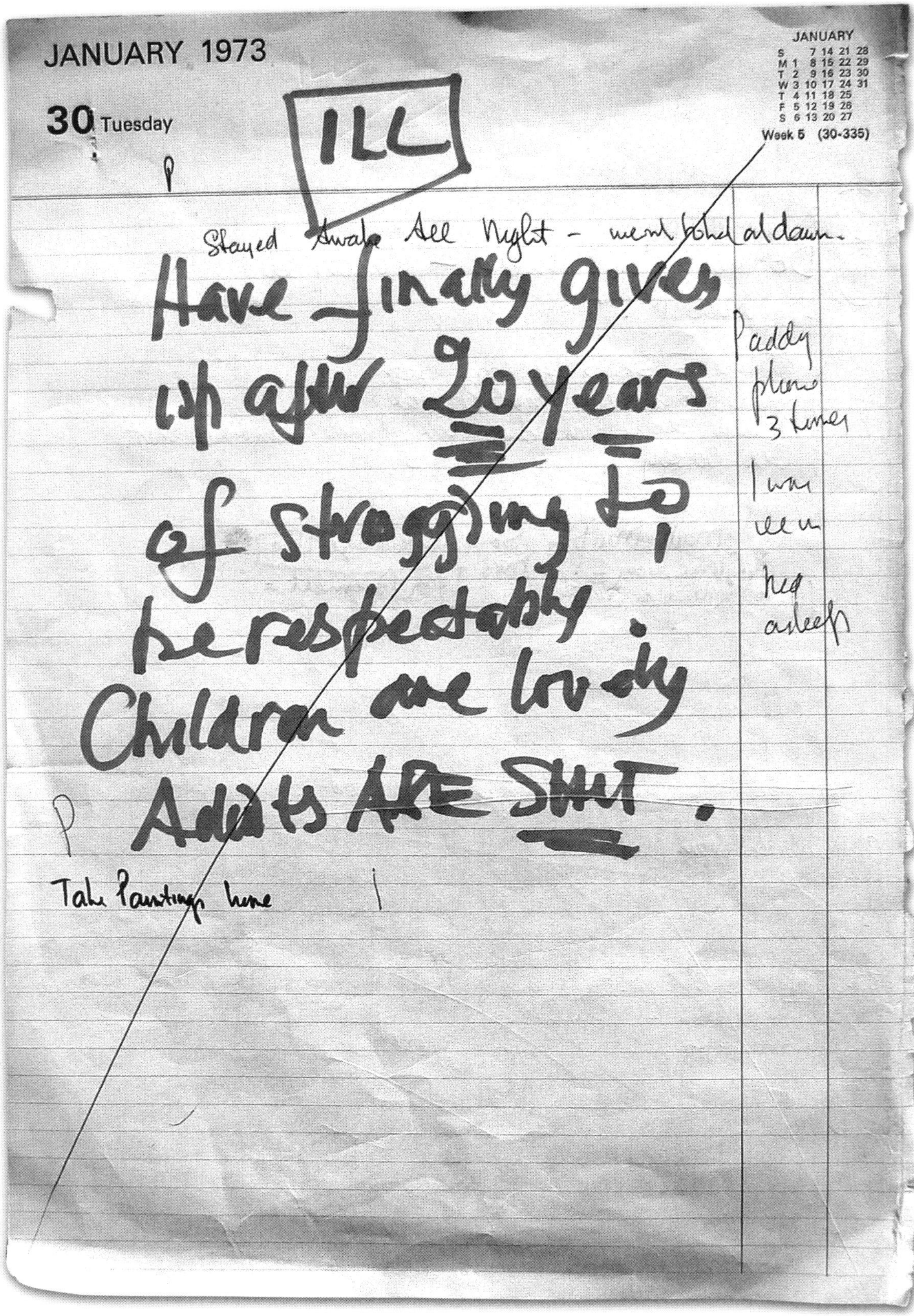

Pure Milligan.

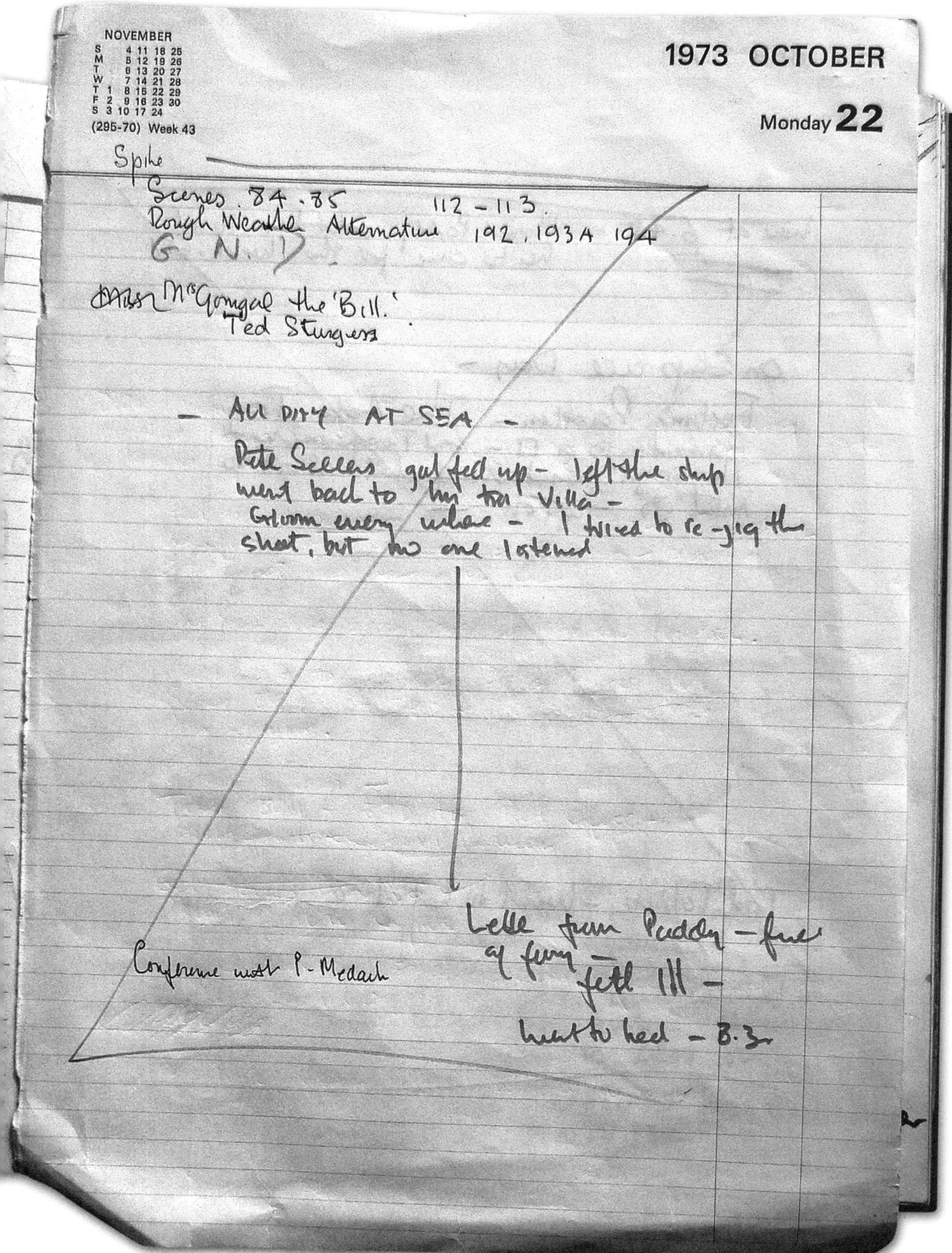

NOVEMBER
S 4 11 18 25
M 5 12 19 26
T 6 13 20 27
W 7 14 21 28
T 1 8 15 22 29
F 2 9 16 23 30
S 3 10 17 24
(295-70) Week 43

1973 OCTOBER

Monday 22

Spike

Scenes 84.85 112 – 113.
Rough Weather Alternative 192, 193 A 194
G. N. 17

Mrs McGonigal the 'Bill.'
Ted Sturgess.

– ALL DAY AT SEA –

Pete Sellers got fed up – left the ship
went back to his Villa –
Gloom every where – I tried to re-jig the
shot, but no one listened

Letter from Paddy – fine
of fury –
felt ill –

went to bed – 8.30

Conference with P. Medak

The film was *Ghost in the Noonday Sun* and we were on location in Kyrenia.

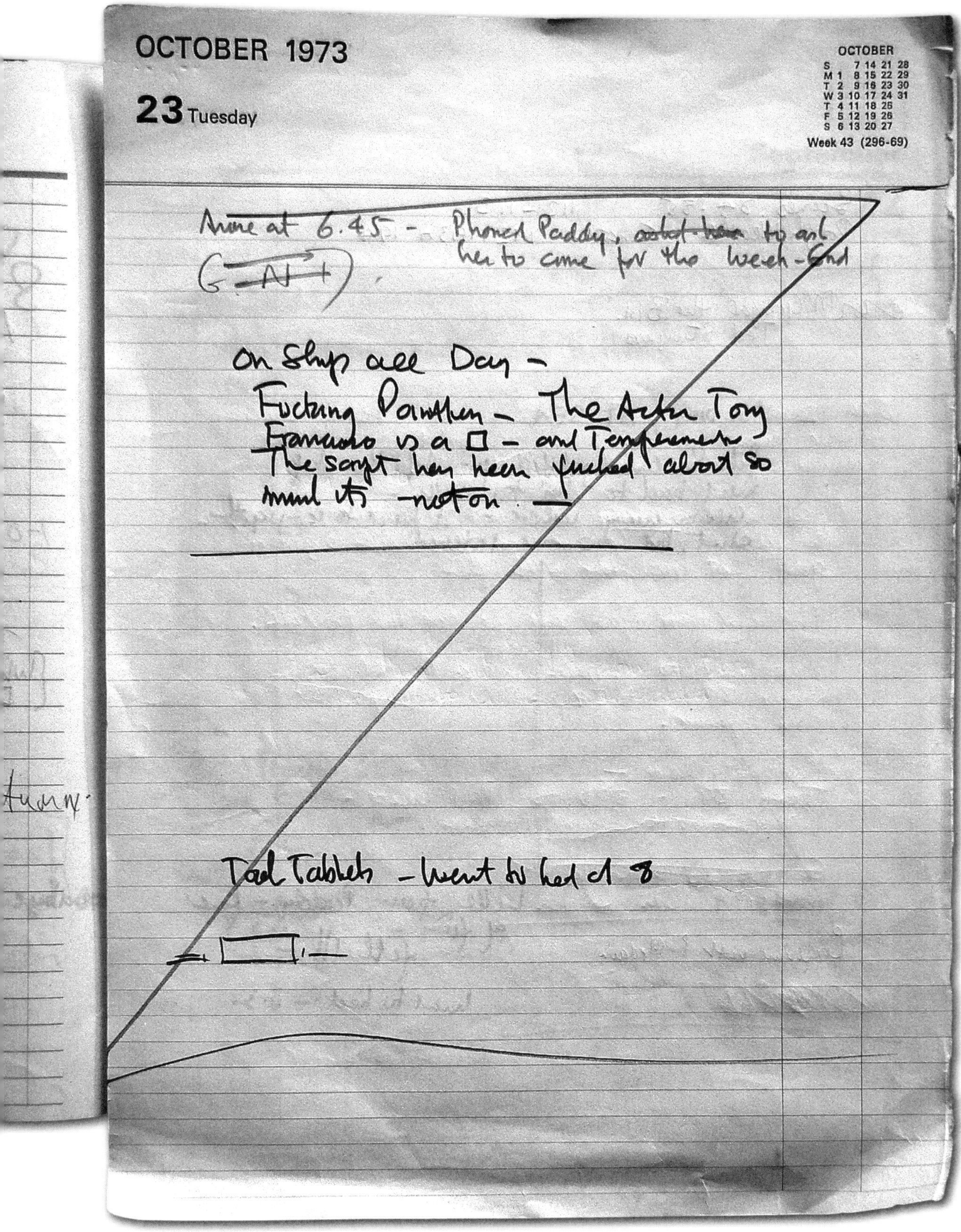

OCTOBER 1973

23 Tuesday

OCTOBER

S		7	14	21	28
M	1	8	15	22	29
T	2	9	16	23	30
W	3	10	17	24	31
T	4	11	18	25	
F	5	12	19	26	
S	6	13	20	27	

Week 43 (296-69)

Awoke at 6.45 – Phoned Paddy, ~~asked her~~ to ask her to come for the week-end

(G-N+)

On Ship all Day –

Fucking Panther – The Actor Tony Franciosa is a □ – and Temperamental

The script has been fucked about so much its not on. —

Took Tablets – went to bed at 8

He was right about the script: it was a disaster. And what about the 'temperamental' bit!

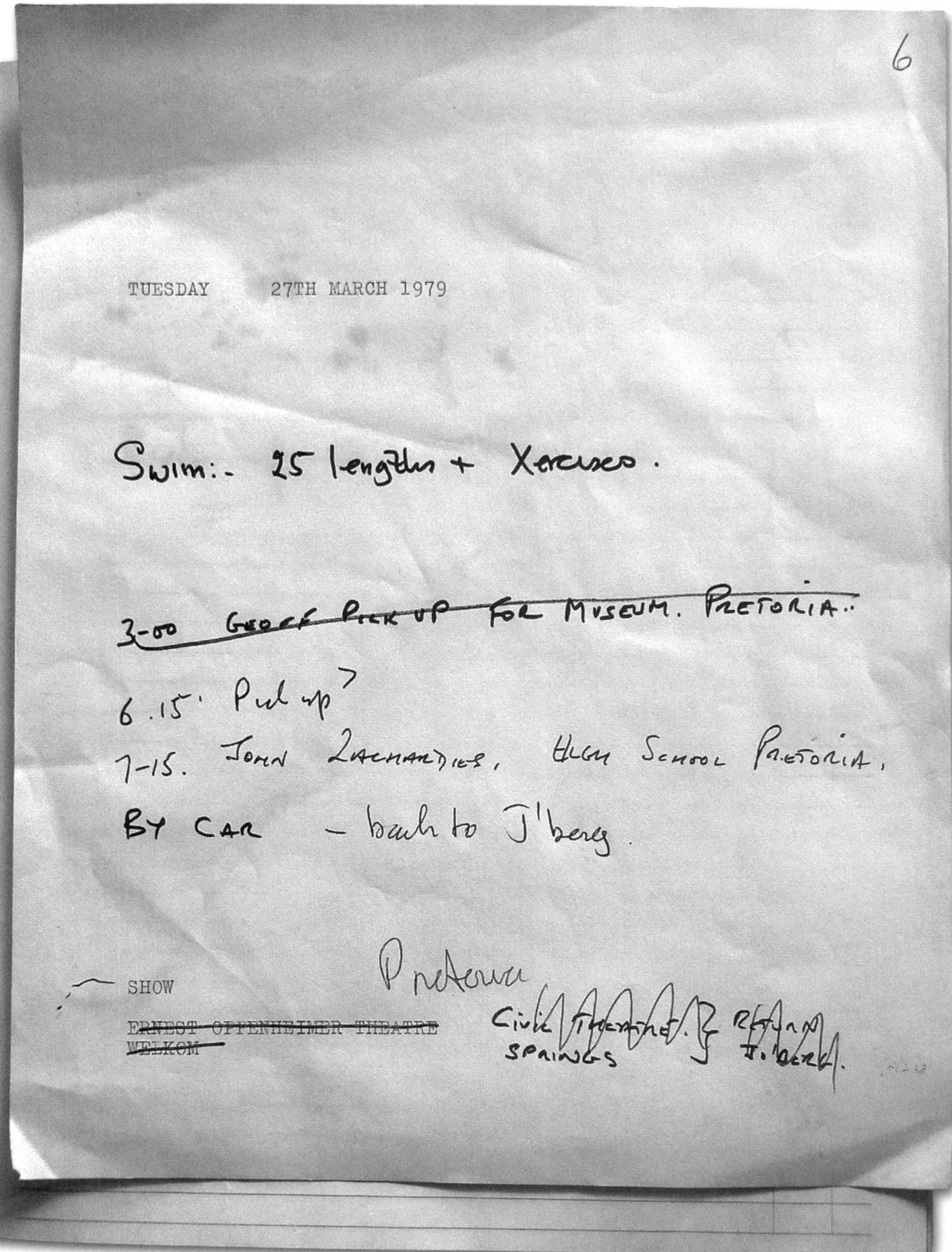

6

TUESDAY 27TH MARCH 1979

Swim:- 25 lengths + Xercises.

~~3-00 Geoff Pick up For Museum. Pretoria..~~

6.15' Pick up?

7-15. John Zacharadies, High School Pretoria,

By car - back to J'berg.

Pretoria

— SHOW

~~ERNEST OPPENHEIMER THEATRE~~
~~WELKOM~~

Civic Theatre. Springs

J'berg.

On tour in South Africa, Spike maintained his fitness regime, even in the heat. One day he swam 100 lengths of the pool. Had I not witnessed it I would never have believed him, and would have put it down to one of his fantasies.

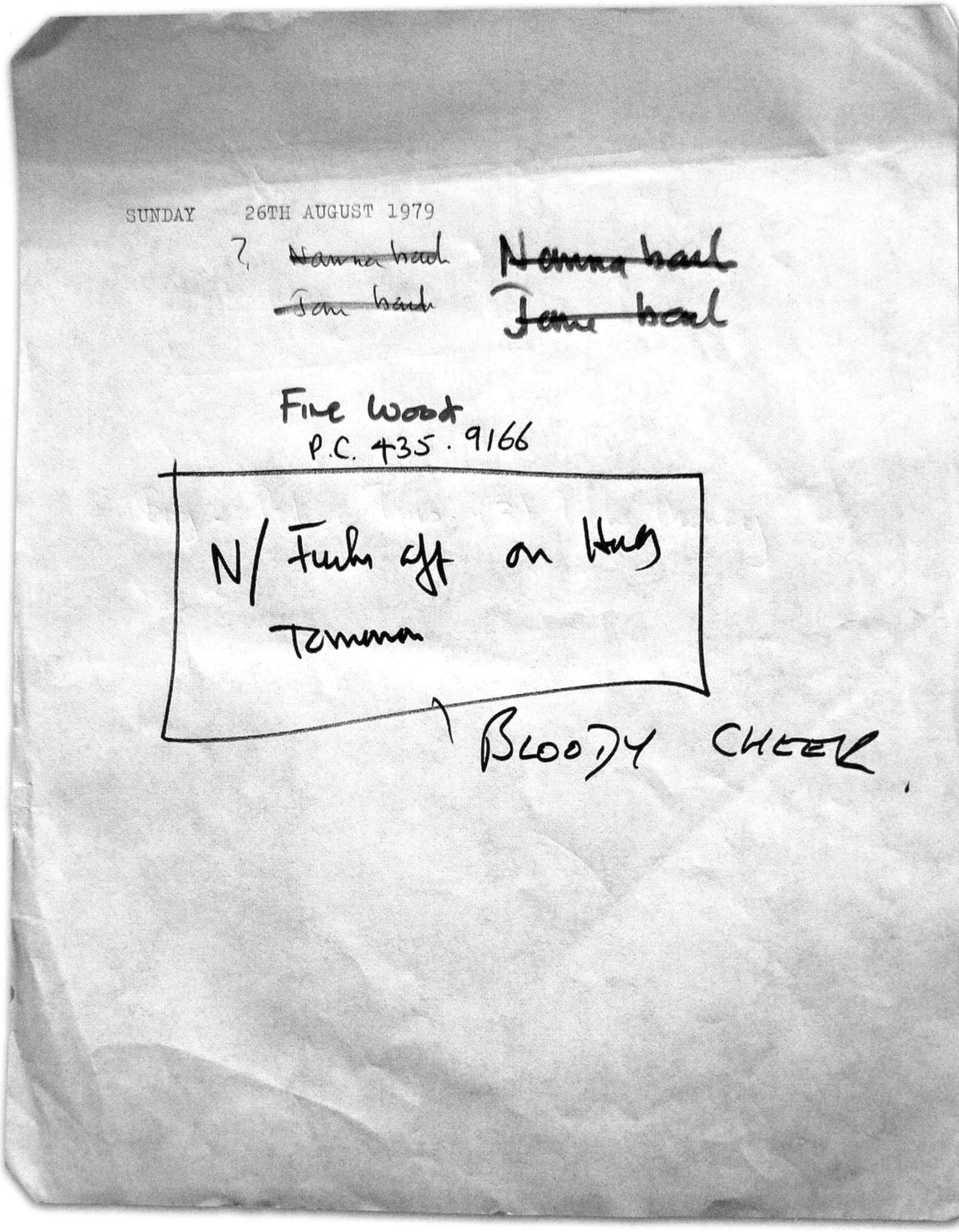

SUNDAY 26TH AUGUST 1979

Fire Wood
P.C. 435 . 9166

N/ Fucks off on Hols
Tomorrow

BLOODY CHEEK.

Me earning a well-deserved rest. Obviously Spike doesn't agree. My comments made him laugh.

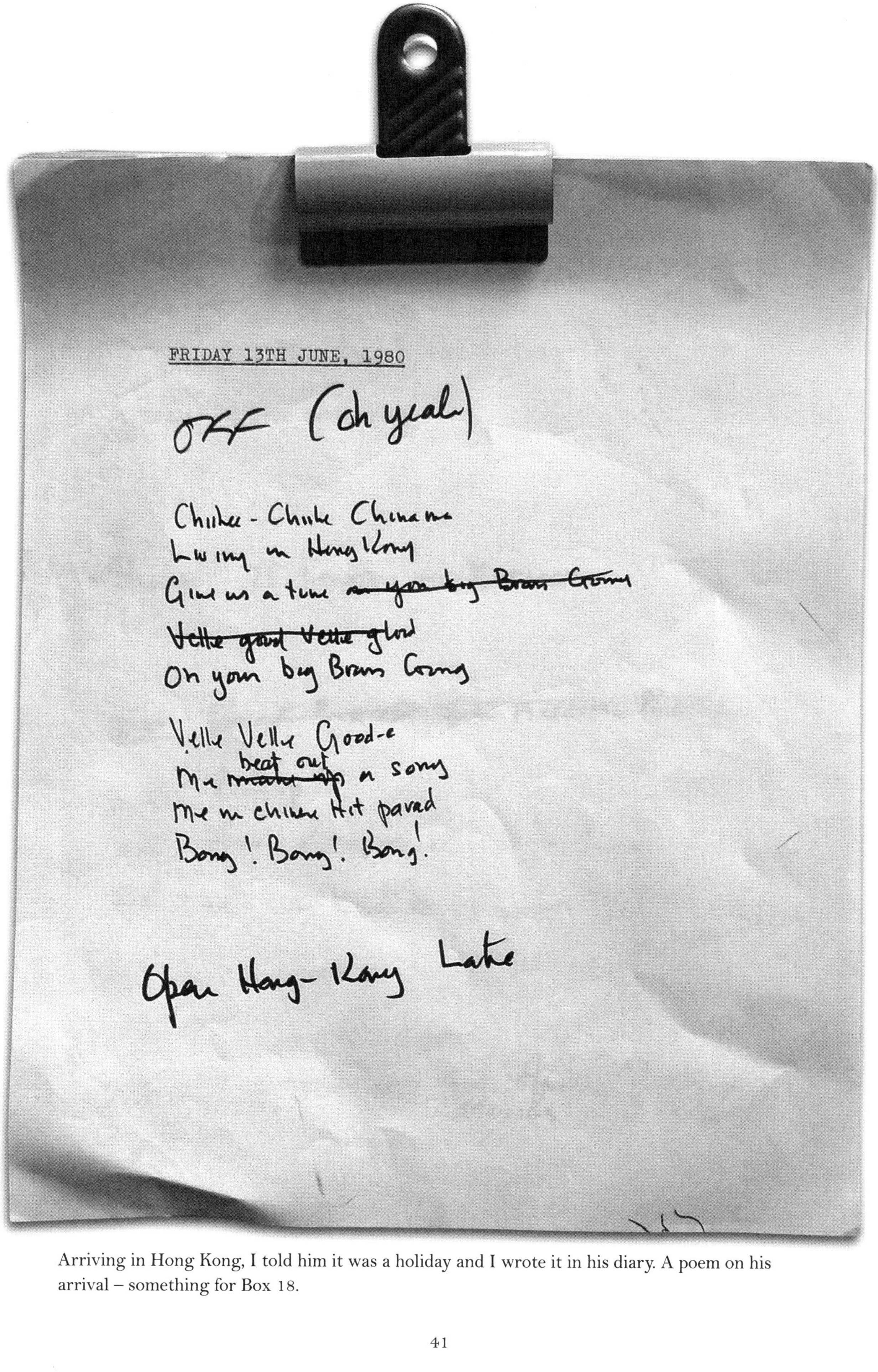

Arriving in Hong Kong, I told him it was a holiday and I wrote it in his diary. A poem on his arrival – something for Box 18.

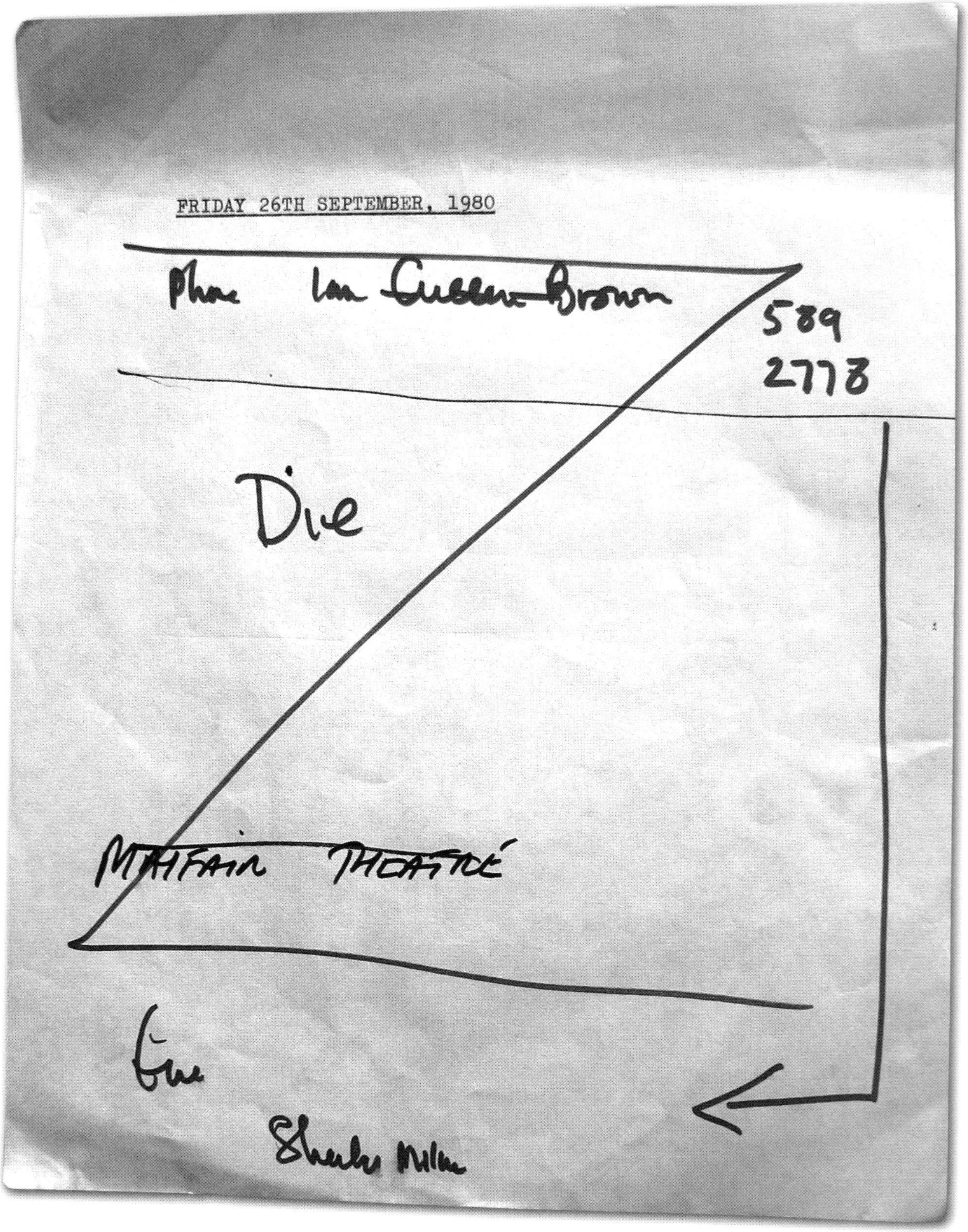

FRIDAY 26TH SEPTEMBER, 1980

Phone Ian ~~[illegible]~~ Brown

589
2778

Die

MAYFAIR THEATRE

He didn't.

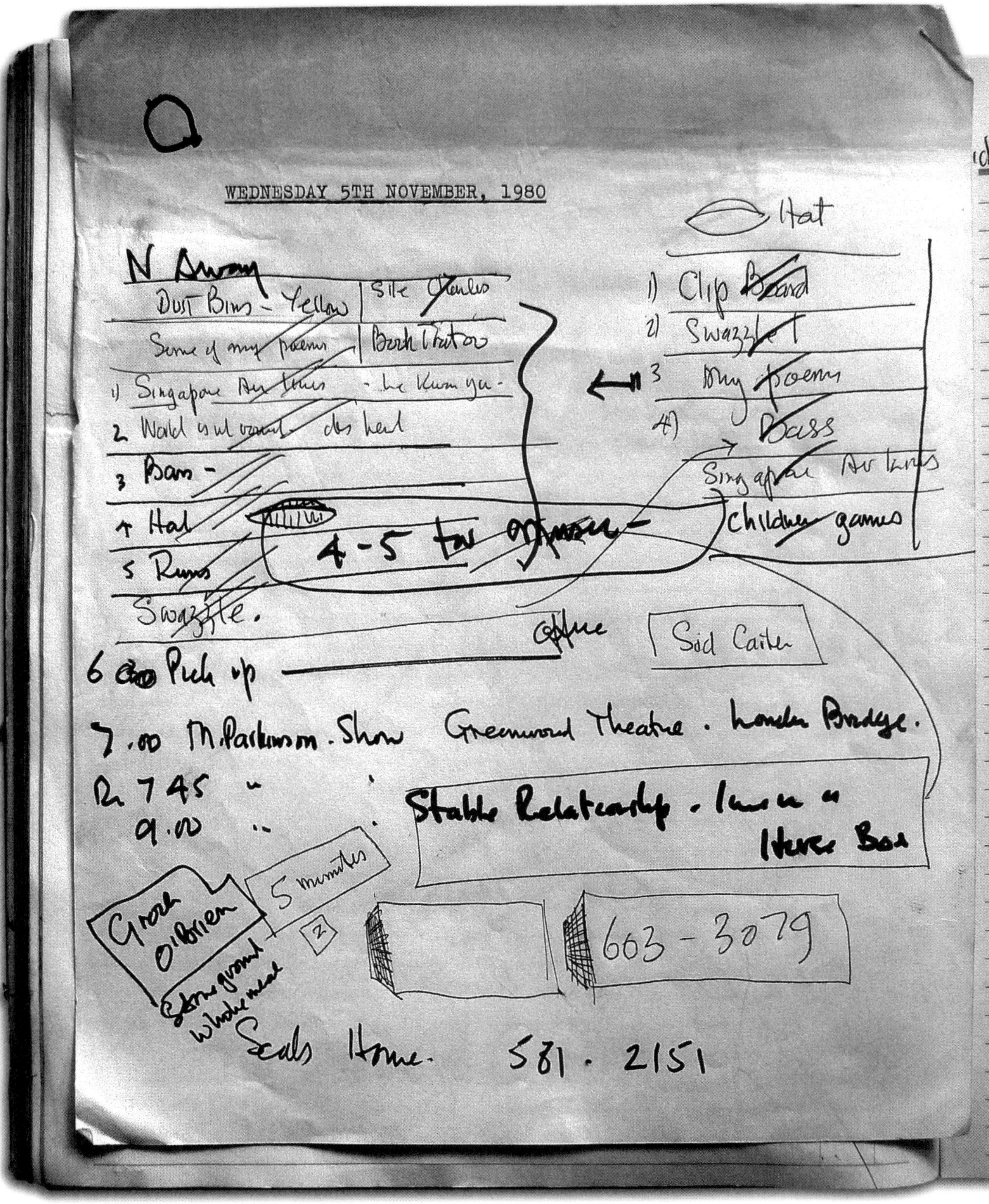

An ordinary day. The crossing-out would indicate that he had achieved what he had set out to do.

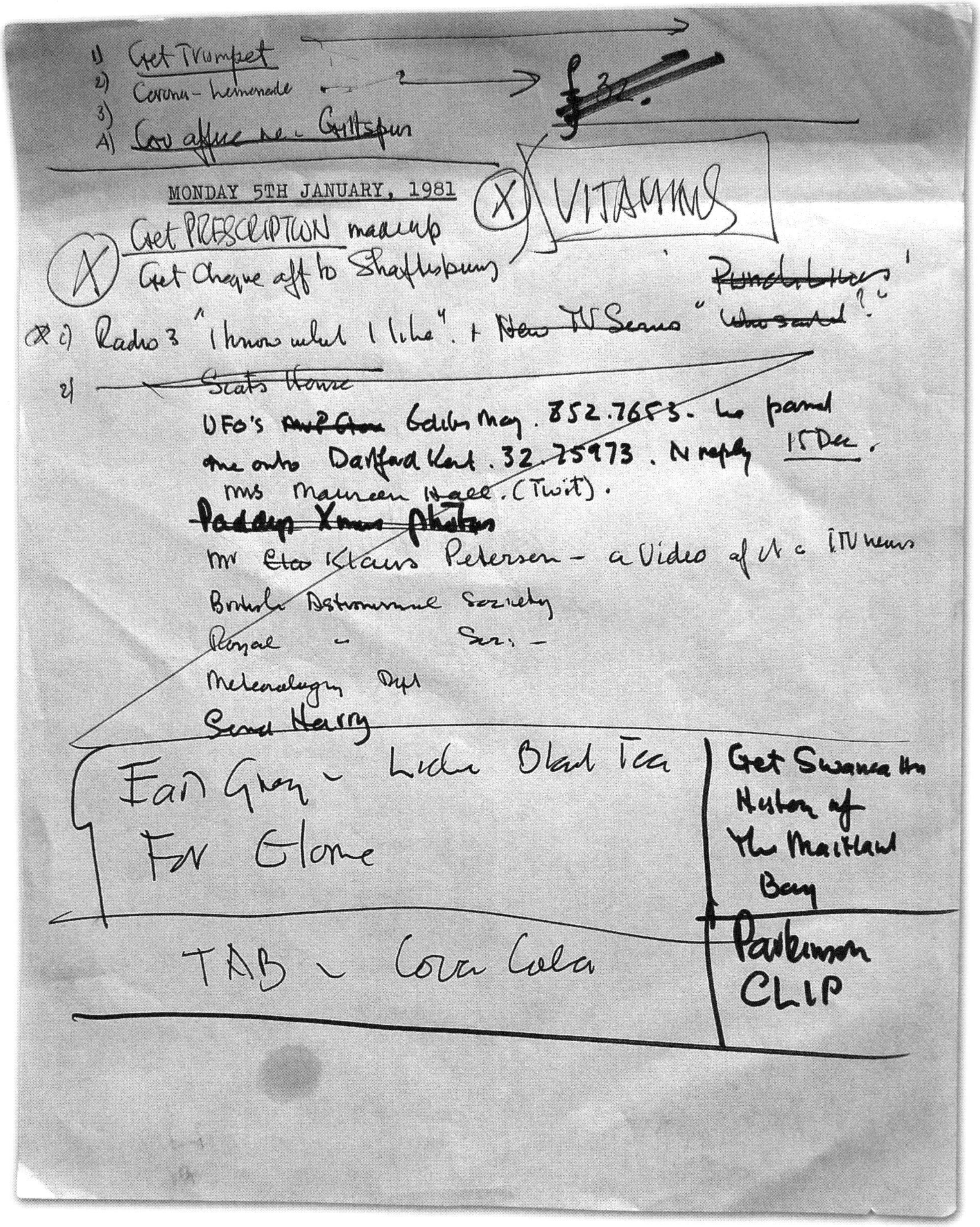
1) Get Trumpet
2) Corona – Lemonade
3)
A) Giltspur
£32.
MONDAY 5TH JANUARY, 1981
VITAMINS
Get PRESCRIPTION made up
Get Cheque off to Shaftesbury
i) Radio 3 "I know what I like". + New TV Series
2) Scats House
UFO's 852.7653.
Dartford Kent. 32.75973. No reply 15 Dec.
Mrs Maureen Hall. (Twit).
Paddy Xmas photos
Mr Klaus Petersen – a Video of the ITV news
British Astronomical Society
Royal – Soc. –
Meteorology Dept
Send Harry
Earl Grey – Black Tea
For Elaine
Get Swansea the History of The Maitland Bay
Parkinson CLIP
TAB – Coca Cola

Another ordinary day – but not for Mrs Maureen Hall, whoever she was. Evidently she was someone who didn't have the information he wanted at that time.

SCRIPTS FOR MILLIGAN'S MILLENNIUM

DUMMY SKETCH

Front room middle class. On the couch is a terrible dummy of a middle aged man. The son is seated on a chair. The mother is knitting.

Son: Mum, Mum.

Mother: Oh what is it now – you've made me drop a stitch.

Son: Mum why did you marry a dummy?

Mother: Lots of reasons, one, he can't answer back, two, if I go and hit him **(she crosses and hits him)** he doesn't complain.

Son: But you can't have children – .

Mother: I had you.

Son: Er – how mother?

Mother: A sperm donor.

Son: You mean my father was a sperm donor.

Mother: One of them.

Son: Which one?

Mother: One called Fred.

Son: Oh, my father was Fred, what was his family name?

Mother: Zakenthrusterbergensteiner Company Limited.

Son: My dad had a limited company?

Mother: Very limited, there was only me.

Son: Is he still alive?

Mother: No.

Son: Is he dead?

Mother: Well they buried him.

Son: Answer the question!

Milligan's Millennium was going to be a TV show produced by my dear friend John Fisher. It never got off the ground, but remained in Box 18.

Dummy Sketch

Front Room middle class. On the couch is a terrible dummy of a middle aged man

The son is seat on a chair.

The mother is knitting.

Son Mum. Mum.

Mother Oh what is it know - you've me drop a stich

Son Mum why did you marry a dummy'

Mother. Lots of reasons, one, he can't answer back two, if I ~~ho hea~~ hit him (she crosses and hits him) he doesn't complain.

Son But you cant have children -

Mother: I had you.

Son Er - how mother

Mother a sperm doner

Son You mean my father was a sperm done

Mother One of them.

Son Which one -

Mother One called Fred

Son Oh, my father was fred, what was his family name

Mother Zakenthrusterberg-en-steiner * Company limited

Son My did had limited Compan?

Mother Very limited. there was only me

Son Is he still alive?

~~Mothe~~ ~~Hes dead~~?

Mother No

Son Is he dead

Mother Well they buried him

Son Answer the question!

Mother Looks at Camera (fade)

Sentry on Duty. Officer approaches.

Officer: 'Good evening, sentry.'

Sentry: 'Good evening, sir.'

Officer: 'Look, don't you salute an officer?'

Sentry: 'No sir.'

Officer: 'Why not?'

Sentry: 'It's my religion. I'm a Catholic – Catholics don't salute officers.'

Officer: 'Who said so?'

Sentry: 'The Pope.'

Officer: 'The Pope? He has no authority to stop you saluting officers.'

Sentry: 'Oh yes he has, sir.'

Officer: 'Who from?'

Sentry: 'God sir, you mustn't disobey God, sir.'

Officer 'Where does it say that?'

Sentry: 'In the Book of Genesis, 'The Lord sayeth that soldiers don't have to salute officers.'

Officer: 'Show me the book.' Sentry hands him the book, officer turns thru the pages. 'It doesn't say it in this book.'

Sentry 'It does, there.' Points to book.

Officer: 'It says "and Abraham sacrificed a ram.'

Sentry: 'Yes, and that translated into Hebrew means you don't have to salute an officer.'

<u>Elephant Substitute</u>

Newspaper Headlines (with dramatic music)

LONDON ZOO RUNS OUT OF ELEPHANTS!
[Search for alternatives]

Cage in zoo. Man with an elephant trunk attached to face.

Visitor, clutching a dummy of a school boy. Speaks to attendant.

Visitor: 'That's not a real elephant.'

Attendant: 'No sir, that's an elephant substitute.'

Visitor: 'You must be joking.'

Attendant: 'No sir, that is a genuine elephant substitute.'

Visitor: 'But I brought my son here to see a real elephant.'

Attendant: 'Is that your son?'

Visitor: 'Yes.'

Attendant: 'Why is he all floppy?'

Visitor: 'He's not a real son, he's a son substitute.

Attendant: [To camera] 'It's a strange world.'

Australian Sketch

London street, into it leaps an Australian (hat with corks), he bounds like a kangaroo. He has a ball and chain round his ankle and wears convict's suit. 'I claim this land fer Orstralia?' He sings

Orstralia - Orstralia
We think of you each day
Orstralia - Orstralia
At work or at play
We think of yew in the morning
And in the evening too
We even wake up at mid-night
So that we can think of you.
Orstralia - Orstralia
We love you from the heart
the kidneys, the liver and the giblets
And every other part.

Policeman: ''ello, 'ello, 'ello, wot are you a doin' of?'

Australian: 'I've just claimed this land as Australia.'

Policeman: 'Then you must have maken a mistake, sir. This place is called England!'

Burst of 'Land of Hope and Glory', police salutes stands to attention.'

Australian: 'England, that's where the Poms come from.'

Policeman: 'Yes.'

Australian: 'Are you a bloody Pom?'

Policeman: 'Yes, I'm a bloody Pom policeman.'

Australian: 'Listen, Rolph Harris lives here, this must be Orstralia.'

Policeman: 'Look, if you don't believe me, I'll take you to see the Queen of England.'

A living room of a working class family. Against one wall the throne of England, on it sits a thirty year old working class frump, wearing the Crown of England.

Policeman pushes door into set. Knocks, a liveried footman answers the door.

Policeman: 'Is the Queen in?'

Footman: 'Yes, she's on the throne at the moment.'

Policeman and Australian go in. There sits a middle class woman in a front room with a throne against the wall.

Policeman: 'Her Majesty, the Queen.' Salutes.

Burst of 'Land of Hope and Glory.' Policeman stands to attention.

Australian: 'Christ, surely you can do better than that'

Policeman: 'Look, she's only a working class Queen. The real Queen lives in Buckingham Palace, but she would meet the likes of you.'

Australian: 'The Bum to the Queen of England' (TO CAMERA)

Footman: 'Ladies and gentlemen, because this man has insulted the Queen, this sketch must end.

Elephant

Line of WC's all vacant except one

Man tries to open door

2 man. Thats in use - its an elephant

man Elephant-? Whats he doing in there

2 man Having a crap

Man A Elephant? He'll smash the, what? seat

2 man Yes. I heard that go - when not one the others?

A

No I've left my watch in ~~them~~ this one.

Man Well I can tell you the time its one-twenty

2 man Hes been in there an hour and a half

Well Suppose and Elephant ~~do~~ does a lot ~~wot~~. to do

Man I'll try and hurry up in there. (knocks on door) Hurry up in there

2 man

Sound of elephant trumpeting

Man Look I've got an appointment - I'll only be 20 min

Could you retrieve my watch

Man 2 Of course

Caption 20 minutes later

Same W.C.s the elephant cubicle is empty

Man returns. Ah! did you get my watch

Man 2 No - he was wearing it.

Exteria Zoo Whipsnade

Ticket office. Ticket man

Man enters: Excuse me one of your elephants is wearing my watch

TM Oh Would you recognise the elephant

Man Oh yes. he'll wearing a watch.

(to camera) I think this as far as you can go in this sketch)

ELEPHANT

Line of WC's all vacant except one.
Man tries to open door

2 Man: That's in use – its an elephant.

Man: Elephant? wots he doing in there

2 Man: Having a crap.

Man: Elephant? He'll smash the bloody seat.

2 Man: Yes I heard that go – why not use one of the others?

Man: No I've left my watch in this one.

2 Man: Well I can tell you the time its one-twenty. He's been in there an hour and a half.

Man: Well I suppose an elephant has a lot to do.

2 Man: I'll try and hurry him up in there **(knocks on door)** Hurry up in there.

Sound of elephant trumpeting

Man: Look I've got an appointment. I'll only be 20 minutes. Could you retrieve my watch?

2 Man: Of course.

Caption 20 minutes later
Same WC's – the elephant cubicle is empty.

Man returns: Ah did you get my watch?

2 Man: No- he was wearing it.

Exterior Zoo Whipsnade
Ticket office. Ticket man

Man enters: Excuse me one of your elephants is wearing my watch

TM: Oh would you recognise the elephant

Man: Oh yes, he'll be wearing a watch
(**to camera** – I think this is as far as you can go in this sketch)

1958: First trip to Australia to appear on ABC Sydney. The show was called *Idiots' Weekly*.

Hitler Job

Job Exchange. Queue. 2nd man in queue is Hitler.

Clerk: 'Hello, I've never seen you here before.'

Hitler: 'No, zis is meine first time.'

Clerk: 'Name?'

Hitler: 'O'Brien, I'm O'Brien.'

Clerk: [Long look]. No you're not. You're Adolph Hitler.'

Hitler: 'Yes.'

Clerk: 'I thought you were dead. It said you blew your brains out in a cellar.'

Hitler: 'Ya, but I missed.'

Clerk: 'Well what are you doin' 'ere?'

Hitler: 'I'm looking for a job.'

Clerk: 'Oh? Wot you want, bricklayer, plumber?

Hitler: 'No, meine old job was Dictator.

Clerk: 'Well we ain't got any vacancies for dictators. I'll put your name down and if one turns up we'll phone. Have you got British citizenship?'

Hitler: 'Listen [sings].

Gott save our gracious Queen,
Long live our noble Queen
Gott save our Queen. Sieg Heil!'

Spike dressed like this for his mother's *This Is Your Life*. There's nothing more to say.

BIBLE SKETCH

Woman dressed as Virgin Mary, comes out of office door

V.Mary: He'll see you now Peter

Interview at Office, behind desk sits Jesus Christ (Chis Langham)
Enter Peter (Spike)

Peter: You wanted to see me Jesus

Jesus: Yes Peter, pull up a chair.

Peter: I'd rather stand.

Jesus: Alright stand on a chair.

Peter: What's this all about Jesus?

Jesus: Peter, listen, when the cock crows three times <u>you</u> will deny me.

Peter: On no I won't

Jesus: Oh yes you will.

Standing by Jesus is a Roman soldier

Roman: Do you know this man?

Peter: No I deny it

This is Good.

Cut to grotty stuffed duck

V: Quack Quack

Peter: That wasn't a cock!

Roman: Do you know this man?

Peter: No I deny it.

Cut to grotty stuffed parrot

V: Pretty polly – pretty polly

Parrot gets hit with a mallet

Me giving Spike my approval – as though he would take any notice.

Bible Sketch, continued:

Peter: That wasn't a cock! Jesus

Roman: Do you know this man

Peter: No I deny it.

Cut to grotty stuffed dog

V: Woof-woof-woof **hit with mallet**

Peter: And **that** wasn't a cock. Jesus.

Jesus: I'm sorry Peter I've been let down by the effects department **(break down)**

Football Referee blows whistle

F.R: Half-time

2-3 minutes

Goon bird

Bible Sketch

Woman dressed as Virgin Mary, comes out of office door

V Mary: Well see you now Peter

Interior of Office, behind desk sits Jesus Christ (Chris Langham)

Enter Peter (Spike) You wanted to see me Jesus

Jesus Yes peter, pull up a chair

Peter I'd rather stand

Jesus Alright stand on a chair

Peter Wots this all about Jesus.

Jesus Peter, listen, when the cock crows three times you will deny me.

Peter Oh no I won't

Jesus Oh yes you will.

Standing by Jesus is a Roman soldier

Roman Do you know this man

Peter No I deny it

Cut to grotty stuffed duck

V. Quack - Quack.

Peter ~~Thats not~~ That wasn't a ~~cock~~! cock.

Roman ~~Doo~~ Do you know this man?

Peter No I deny it.

Cut to Grotty stuffed parrot

V Pretty Polly - pretty polly. (S) THIS IS GOOD. YOU CAN OPEN ON THIS

Parrot gets hit with a mallet

Peter That wasn't a cock! Jesus.

Roman Do you know this man

Peter No - I ~~denyed~~ deny it.

Cut to grotty stuffed dog

Woof - Woof - Woof hit with mallet

Peter And that wasn't a cock Jesus

(~~Groucho Marx. Don't believe all you read in the Bible~~.)

Jesus: I'm sorry Peter I've been let down by the effects department (breaks down)

Football referee, blows whistle

'F.R.' Half-time

2-3 mins

My way of trying to encourage him.

Virgin Mary comes out door: 'Alright you can go in now, Peter.'

Peter goes in. Jesus is sitting behind desk. A man stands behind him.

Peter: 'You wanted to see me, Jesus?'

Jesus: 'Yes Peter, when the cock crows three times you will deny it.'

Peter: 'Oh no I won't.'

Jesus: 'Oh yes you will.'

Grotty parrot squawks three times.

Man points to Jesus: 'Do you know this man?'

Peter: 'No.'

Jesus: 'You see?'

Peter: 'That wasn't a cock, it was a parrot.'

Jesus: 'Oh no it wasn't.'

Peter: 'Oh yes it was.'

Jesus: 'When the cock crows three times you will deny me.'

Grotty parrot squawks three times.

Man to Peter: 'Do you know this man?'

Peter: 'No. I deny it.'

Soldier Sketch

Soldier: 'I am a soldier, I shoot people. Ah, there's one now. Bang!'

Man: 'Oh oh oh oh - ow owo Oh-oh ah.'

Soldier: 'This man is going for the over acting award of the year.'

Policeman: 'ello, 'ello, 'ello, wot's a goin on 'ere?' I be of assistance? A mouth to mouth, or heart resuscitation?'

Man: 'That man has just killed me.'

Policeman: 'That is a very serious charge. Have you any evidence of the occurrence?'

Man: 'Yes, this, my death certificate.'

Policeman: 'This will come in very useful at the enquiry.

In Court.

Judge: 'The victim appears to be proper dead alive.'

Solicitor: 'Yes, my client is waiting for the case to end to be proper dead[?]'

Judge: 'You - you killed this man, do you plead guilty, or not guilty?'

Man: 'Oh, I've got a choice, I'll go for not guilty.'

Judge: 'Go, I get home early for dinner - we got spaghetti rings tonight.'

Cat - Coffin

Front door.

RSPCA man knocks.

Door opens by a housewife.

Housewife:	'Yes?'
RSPCA:	'Good morning madam, I'm from the RSPCA. I've come to make arrangements in the event of your cat dying.
Woman:	'Oh, what do you want to do?'
RSPCA:	'Measure him for a cat - coffin.'
Woman:	'It's a strange request - but come in.'

RSPCA man comes in with three different-sized small cat - coffins. Picks up a floppy stuffed cat.

RSPCA:	'Can I just try your cat on one?' (Picks up cat, tries it in the box). 'Perfect! Do you want the cat tail included?'
Woman:	'You're not going to cut it off are you?'
RSPCA:	'Oh no madam - but the tail will need an extension to the box (puts extension for tail to coffin). 'Perfect. Now would you like to pay for it in advance?'
Woman:	'No, he isn't dead yet.'
RSPCA:	'Well you don't want to wait til the last moment.'
Woman:	'Yes I do. Actually I'm waiting for the last moment.'

Two Egyptologists with torches walking in an underground tomb. Suddenly they come upon a casket with Egyptian hieroglyphics.

1st Egyptian: 'My God, Sanders, this is it?' (He reads hieroglyphics). "Here lies the body of Im-oth-the II Pharoah of all Egypt." Carefully they lift the lid, then gasp.

1st Egyptian: We're too late - he's dead!'

Corny chord from Orchestra.

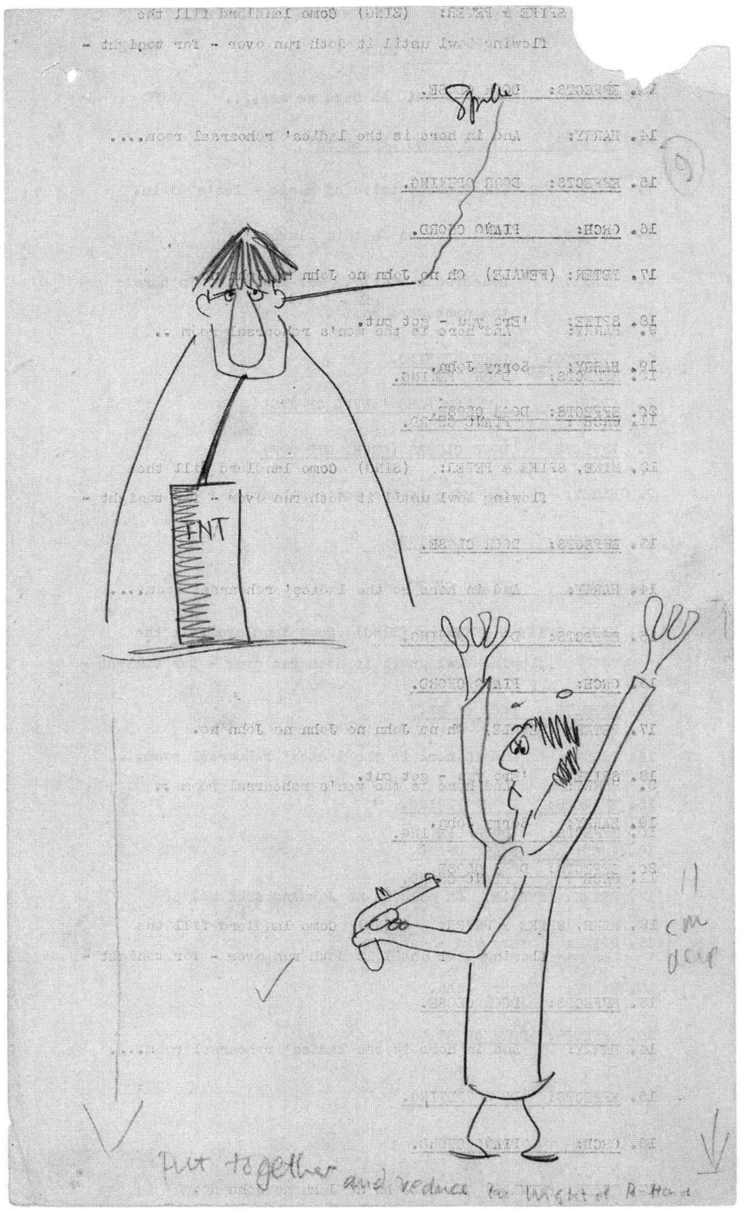

<u>The Cliffs. Brighton</u>

[V.O.] Man standing at cliff edge enjoying the view-

Caption: Man Standing on the Cliffs, Brighton enjoying the view.

2nd Man 'Excuse me interrupting, are you going to be standing here long?'

1st Man 'No, why?'

2nd Man 'My mother-in-law wants to commit suicide from here.'

1st Man 'Oh, didn't you try to stop her?'

2nd Man 'No, in fact it was I who suggested it.'

1st Man 'Why does she want to commit suicide?'

2nd Man 'Because I suggested it.'

1st Man 'Is she going to jump?'

2nd Man 'No, she's taking aspirin.'

1st Man 'That won't kill her.'

2nd Man 'She's taking ten thousand.'

Optican

So man comes into Opticans shop

Optican. Yes sir what can I do for you

Man Can I see an optican

Optican Not with out glass sir

man You ~~see~~ I-I-can't see

optican Thats why you can't see an optican

man I can't see at all

Optican Oh- come out side sir

OUTSIDE

~~Outside~~ Hand holds out sign

Optican Now sir look up

Man Do I have too

Optican Yes

(man looks up)

Optican Can you see the sun

man Yes.

Optican How bloody far do you want to see

Man I only want to see as Far as Doris Watson

Optican Why

man Shes got big boobs.

Op~~tican Oh~~

man ~~If not I want to see her mother Rita~~

Opt~~ican Why~~

man ~~She got bigger boobs~~

Optican I sorry we don't have that type of glasses

man What type have you got

Optican These (Hands him two pint glasses)

man Holds them up like binoculars

Optican Can you see anything

man Yes I can see you - but you haven't got big boobs.

OPTICIAN

Man comes into optician's shop

Optician: Yes sir what can I do for you?

Man: Can I see an optician?

Optician: Not without glasses sir.

Man: You see I-I- can't see.

Optician: That's why you can't see an optician.

Man: I can't see at all.

Optician: Oh- come outside sir.

Hand holds out sign OUTSIDE

Optician: Now sir look up.

Man: Do I have to.

Optician: Yes

(Man looks up)

Optician: Can you see the sun?

Man: Yes

Optician: How bloody far do you want to see?

Man: I only want to see as far as Doris Watson

Optician: Why

Man: She's got big boobs.

Optician: I'm sorry we don't have that type of glasses.

Man: What type have you got?

Optician: These **(hands him two pint glasses)**.

Man holds them up like binoculars

Optician: Can you see anything?

Optician sketch, continued

Man: Yes I can see you – but you haven't got big boobs

Optician: Sorry

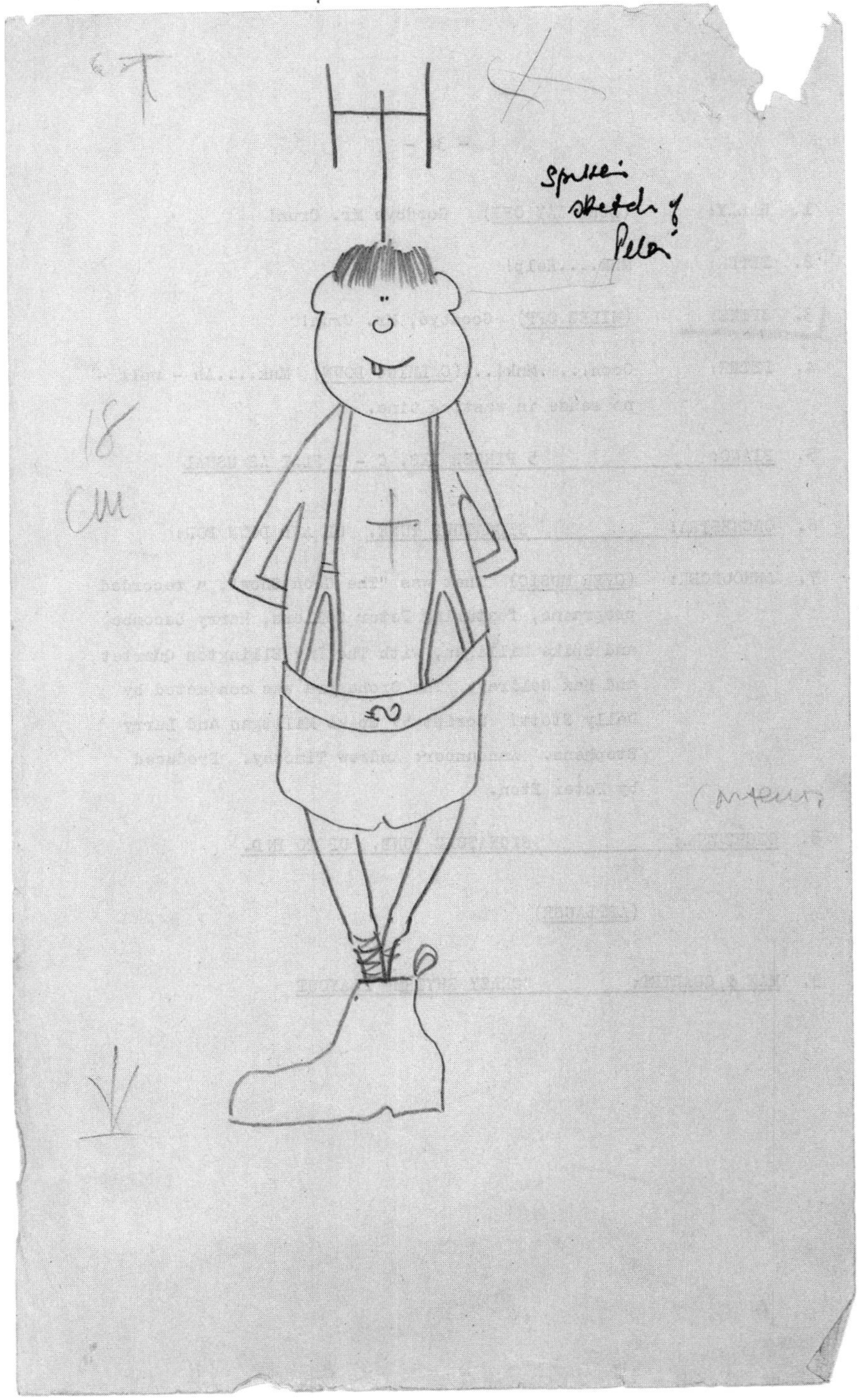

Milligan Preserved LP. Spike, John Antrobus, Valentine Dyall and Paddy Milligan.

Around 1945 or 1946: A rare photo of the Bill Hall Trio. Alexander Club, Rome. The start of it all.

HERMAN GORING

87

Herman Goring found himself driving a No 112A bus to Catford. Wot in Gods name am I doing driving a No 112A bus to Catford, No I should be broadcasting Nazi propaganda on Radio Berlin. A British Bobby halted the bus, he approach the driving cab and said 'Herman Goring I arrest you for bein a Nazi, and a danger to the Royal Family' "How can I harm zer Royal Family, zey have Iron railing around the Palace, and a Sentry on guard with a bearskin and a loaded rifle.." "I must ask you to come down to the Station. Meekly Goring obeyed. and ended up in a cell 12 foot by ten, with another prisoner who was drunk and being sick. 'This is an insult to me' he shouted thru the bars, I'm used to sumptious living, in zer grand manner" 'Well fuck you Jack" said a Police Sergeant' Handing him a plate of beans and porridge. "I can't eat zis crap' he said 'You dont have too' said the Bobby' You can keep it" 'I'll keep it in zer fridge' said Goring 'It vill keep longer". The fridge was broken, the whole meal came out covered in mildew, but Goring was hungry he ate the meal mildew and all, but an hour later, he started to go green, a Green Goring was something to behold, he hid this by spraying him flesh pink, he stood out in a crowd. he even stood out on his own.

Fuck zis for a life' he swore.

"You know Herman' said his wife 'I find you most attractive in pink"

Good this promises some extra fucks

Please, no letters telling me this has been published before. I can't find it – so, OK, it definitely hasn't been published in Spike's handwriting before. 10/10, Norma.

HERMAN GORING found himself driving a No 112A bus to Catford.

Wot in Gods name am I doing driving a No 112A bus to Catford, No I should be broadcasting Nazi propaganda on Radio Berlin.

A British Bobby halted the bus. he approach the driving cab and said 'Herman Goring I arrest you for been a Nazi, and a danger to the Royal Family'

'How can I harm zer Royal Family, zey have iron railing around the Palace, and a Sentry on guard with a bearskin and a loaded rifle.

'I must ask you to come down to the Station. Meekly Goring obeyed, and ended up in a cell 12 foot by ten, with another prisoner who was drunk and being sick.

'This is an insult to me' he shouted thru the bars, I'm used to sumptuous living, in zer grand manner'

'Well, fuck you luck' said a Police Sergeant Handing him a plate of beans and porridge

'I can't eat zis crap' he said

'You don't have too' said the Bobby 'You can keep it.'

'I'll keep it in zer fridge' said Goring 'It vill keep longer.'

The fridge was broken, the whole meal came out covered in mildew, but Goring was hungry he ate the meal mildew and all, but an hour later, he started to go green, a Green Goring was something to behold, he hid this by spraying him flesh pink, he stood out in a crowd . . . he even stood out on his own

Fuck zis for a life' he swore.

'You know Herman' said his wife 'I find you most attractive in pink'

Good this promises some extra fucks

Meantime on the farm Hitler was feeding the pigs 'Jewish swine' he bellowed at them. The pigs were not moved. 'You all look like the swine Churchill. I'll make him pay for zis war.'

Churchill had no intention in paying for the war. At that moment Churchill was tucking into roast phesant and chips while drinking a vintage Burgundy I wonder what that Nazee bastard is doing. I would think that at this time of night he would be thinking of screwing Eva Braun, said his man servant.

'I hope she gives him a dose' growled the great man, pouring himself some rare old brandy 'Couldn't win the war with a this stuff.'

We certainly could all do with a good stuff' said his man servant.

'Tell my secretary Miss Dobson, to prepare for one.'

An hour later Churchill lifted himself off Miss Dobson pouring with sweat. 'How much will that be Miss Dobson.'

As it was in my free time, a hundred and ten pounds.

He wrote out a cheque for the amount. 'Just give me time to get out of the country'

Cheque was returned 'Insufficient funds'.

Bugger said Miss Dobson 'I've been fucked for nothing' To cover himself he gave her an IOU. 'When will this become due' said Miss Dobson.

'Christmas,' said Churchill.

'Christmas?' said Miss Dobson. 'That ten bloody months away.'

'So it is' said Churchill

'I can't wait that long' said Miss Dobson.

'Well, I can,' said Churchill and buggered off. He went to ten Downing Street as he live there rent free. Churchill was short of money all of his life, and even after that

'Darling, you must stop buying black silk underwear' said Clementine.

'Why' said Churchill 'no one can see them'!

'They're too expensive dear.'

'Look' said Churchill 'I'm Prime Minister of England, if I can't afford it, who can? eh? eh?'

'But at the end of the month we're broke' said Clementine.

'Oh, I've been in tighter spots than that' he laughed.

'Well were overdrawn at the bank by ten thousand pounds'

'Well, I've been in tighter spots than that' he said lighting a Havana Cigar and sipping a brandy. 'Lord Beaverbrook is going to give me ten thousand pounds for writing an article on life in the Artic' he said.

'Youve never been to the Artic' said Clementine

'Ah but he does'nt know that, said Churchill

'That's cheating' said Clementine stamping her foot, and breaking her ankle 'Now look what you've made me do' she said limping away.

88

Meantime on the farm Hitler was feeding the pigs 'Jewish swine' he bellowed at them. The ~~pigs~~ pigs were not moved. 'You all look like the swine ~~Churchill~~ Churchill. ~~Churchill~~. I'll make him pay for this war'. Churchill had no intention in paying for the war. At that moment Churchill was tucking into roast phesant and ~~chipp~~ chips while drinking a vintage Burgundy 'I wonder what that Nazee bastard is doing. I would think that at this time of night he would be thinking of screwing Eva Braun, said his man servant. I hope she gives him a dose.' growled the great man. pouring himself some rare old brandy' Could win the war with a this stuff'. 'We certainly could all do with a good stuff said his man servant.' Tell my secretary Miss Dobson, to prepare for one'. An hour later Churchill lifted himself off Miss Dobson pouring with sweat.' How much will that be Miss Dobson. As it was in my free time, a hundred and ten pounds. He wrote out a cheque for the amount.' Just give me time to get out of the country' Cheque was returned' Insuffient funds'. Bugger said Miss Dobson' I've been fucked for nothing' To cover himself he gave her an IOU. 'When will this become due' said Miss ~~Dobson~~ Dobson. 'Christmas' said ~~Churc~~ Churchill. 'Christmas?' said Miss Dobson' That ten bloody months away 'So it is' said Churchill' I can't wait that long' said Miss Dobson. 'Well, I can said Churchill and buggerd off. He went to ten Downing Street as he lived there rent free. Churchill was short of money all of his life, and even after that

Note: words missed out and words not completed – Spike would give this version to me to 'do whatever you have to do with it'. Most often with a note: 'Please ignore spelling – I did.'

'Darling, you must stop buyin black silk underwear' said Clemtine. 'why' said Churchill, 'no one can see them'! 'Theyre too expensive dear'! 'Look' said Churchill 'Im Prime Minister of England, if I cant afford it, who can? eh? eh?' 'But at the end of the month were broke' said Clemtine. 'Oh we've been in tighter spots than that' he laughed. 'Well were overdrawn at the bank by ten thousand pounds' 'Well we've been in tighter spots than that' he said lighting a Havana Cigar and sipping a brandy. 'Lord Beaverbrook is going to give me ten thousand pounds for writing an article on life in the Artic' he said.

'Youve never been to the Artic' said Clemtine

'Ah but he doesn't know that' said Churchill

'Thats cheating' said Clemtine stamping her foot, and breaking her ankle. 'Now look what you've made me do' she said limping away. 'I didnt make you do it' growled Churchill. 'Youd better lie down' he suggested. 'Wat good that do' she said. 'It will get you out of the bloody way' he said pushing her back. Just then came the drone of German plane.

'Quick phone the RAF and tell them to shoot it down.' A bomb landed next to Churchill and blew him backward out of his boots thru a window, he landed on a dustman in the act of emptying a bin 'Cor Blimey Winston Churchill' he gasped 'wat a way to meet you'

'The smell of the dustman drove Churchill away

'Bloody snob' shouted the dustman after him. Churchill shouted something back but was too far away to be heard it was in fact the words 'Bollocks'

'I did'nt make you do it growled Churchill. 'You'd better lie down' he suggested.

Wat good that do? she said

'It will get you out of the bloody way' he said pushing her back. Just then came the drone of German plane. 'Quick, phone the RAF and tell them to shoot it down.

A bomb landed next to Churchill and blew him backward out of his boots thru a window, he landed on a dustman in the act of emptying a bin 'Cor Blimey Winston Churchill' he gasped 'Wat a way to meet you'

'The smell of the dustman drove Churchill away

'Bloody snob' shouted the dustman after him.

Churchill shouted something back but was to far away to be heard it was in fact the word 'Bollocks'

Of course, thousands of miles away, Gandhi was resting and fasting and dying after his salt march to the sea he was laying on a rush mat in a room at the Indian YMCA.

'You must eat or you will die' said his European follower Mrs Gladys Squirt

'Thank you for the warning' said Gandhi collapsing to the floor

'Here eat this mango' she said

'They give you boils' said Gandhi

'Not right away' she said ramming one down his throat,

choking, he coughed up the stone'.

'Im sorry I forgot to take out' she said to the unconscious figure on the floor, with hot baths, massage, electric shock treatment and a five course meal Gandhi recovered enough to sit up and play play with himself. I must save India 'he said first we must kill all the whites.'

'I thought you were non violent' she said, kissing his feet

'While your down there can you cut my toe nails'

'I have'nt any scissors' she said

'Then bite them off'

'Im not biting any wogs toe nails' she retorted, tossing her head and catching as it came down

'Whats life about' said Nehru.

'Its about 70 for women and 65 for men' she said.

Of course, thousands of miles away, Ghandi was 90
resting ~~and~~ fasting and dying after his salt march to the sea,
he was laying on a rush mat in a ~~room~~ room
at the Indian YMCA. "You must eat or you will die'
said his European follower Mrs Gladys Squirt, "Thank
you for the warning' said Ghandi collapsing to the floor
'Here eat this mango' she said 'They give you
boils' said Ghandi " ; Not ~~for a while~~ right away ' she said
ramming one down his throat; choking he coughed
up the stone' 'I'm sorry I forgot to ~~take~~ take
out' she said to the unconscious figure on
the floor, with hot baths, massage,
electric shock treatment and a five course meal
Gandhi recovered enough to sit ~~up~~ up and play Play
with himself.. I must save India ' he said . 'I thought
first we must kill all the whites.
you were non violent," she said kissing his
feet 'While you down there can you cut my
toe nails," 'I have not any scissors' she said
'Then bite them off" "I'm not biting any woops
toe nails' she retorted, tossing her head
and catching as it came down ' whats
life about' said Nehru, "about 70 for women
and 65 for men' she said. Nehru realised
he was ~~65~~ 65 so immediately dropped down
dead "One down ten to go' said Mhatma
placing Nehru on a pyre setting fire to
it and floated it down the Ganges
he floated out to sea where he
was hit by SS Mary and sank
nearly the boat. The heat from
the fire revived him, and he
rowed the burning pyre back
to the shore, where he was treated
for burns and malaria and
starvation, he went on eat
anything said he was slimming
loosing 20 pounds a day
on the 7th day he disappeared
But reappear a month later in
a nun cell in the convent
of Jesus & Mary, Poona

Nehru realised he was 65 immediately dropped down dead.

'One down ten to go said Mhatma, placing Nehru on a pyre setting fire to it and floated it down the Ganges he floated out to sea where he was hit by SS Mary and sank not him, the boat. The heat from the fire revived him, and he rowed the burning pyre back to the shore, where he was treated for burns and malaria and starvation, he would'nt eat anything said he was slimming loosing 20 pounds a day on the seventh day he dissappeared But reappear a month later in a nun cell in the convent of Jesus Mary, Poona

The nun was in bed and took the opportunity of dragging him in and screwing 'That's better,' she said 'Better' he said theres never been anything wrong with it'. Well he had now because she'd given him a dose. Shes a bloody Catholic! Three injections of Penicillin cleared the dose. But he swore never to co-habit with a nun again. Out of boredom he stowed away on a tramp steamer crewed by a mixture of far eastern cut-throat, They did'nt cut his throat but screwed the ass off him, in desperation he dived overboard and swam ashore and landed on a cannibal island where he was boiled and eaten with chips. His son Don came searching for him, he was very skinny, so was captured by the cannibals and put on a full fat diet, in preparation for boiling and eaten, alas he worried so much he never fattened, so they let him go, but where to go, he chose his native land Ireland he was welcomed home by a crowd of Irish idiots, recently released from the asylum due to over crowding.

'Come wid me Ive someting to show you' He showed him teapot, it was someting but that was all

'Its not very interesting' he said hitting the Irish idiot he didn't know that the idiot was a Karate expert, and ended up hurled into a tree, 'Get me down,' he shouted so the idiot sawed thru the branch Don was sitting on till it collapsed, crashing Don to the ground – and a hospital Alas the hospital was Pychaitric full of loonies, and tried to sell his bed to him for a million pounds

THE END

The nun was in bed and took the opportunity of dragging
him in and screwing "Thats better," she said' Better' he said
theres never been anything wrong with it'. Well he had now knew
she'd given him a dose. Shes a bloody Catholic! Three
injections of Penicillin cleared the dose. But he swore never
~~he could~~ to co-habit with a nun again. Out of boredom
he stowed away on a tramp steamer crewed by a mixture
of far eastern cut-throats, they didnt cut his throat but
screwed the arse off him, in desperation he dived overboard
and swam ashore and landed on a cannibal island
where he was boiled and eaten with chips. His son
Don came searching for him, he was very skinny.
so was captured by the cannibals and put on
a full fat diet, in preparation for boiling and
eaten, alas he worried so much he never
fattened, so they let him go, but where
to go, he chose his native land Ireland
he was welcomed home by a crowd of
Irish idiots, recently released from
the asylum due to over crowding
"Come with me' Ive something to show you'
He showed him teapot, it was something
but that was all" Its not very interesting'
he said hitting the Irish idiot, he didnt
know that the idiot was a Karate
expert, and ended up hurled into
a tree, 'Get me down' he shouted
~~Q~~ so the idiot sawed through
the ~~brand~~ branch Don was sitting on
till it collapsed, crashing
Don to the ground - and hospital
Alas the hospital was phychiatric
full of loonies, one tried to
sell his bed to him for a
million pounds

57

His office: I called it his womb. It was chaos but he knew exactly where everything was.

1956: Chatham Empire. Peter, Spike and Max Geldray.

Spike and Eric in their office (collar and ties), 1954. They shared an office for 50 years.

STORIES FOR CHILDREN

THE GREAT BIM-BOM Childrens Circus.

Every ~~boda~~ body at the Bim-bom Childrens Circus
was very excited they were going to perform
at London Towns ~~Hampst~~ famous Hampstead
Heath - the seats were full of children
who were full of jelly babies - suddenly
the Bim-Bom band struck up under its ~~leader~~
conductor Fred Nose, Omm pah-pah went
the Tuba played by Dick Twit, Tootely Toot
went Doris Cabbage, on the flute, she blew
so hard the elastic in her knickers broke and
they fell down - then Ben Barmy the drummer
hit his bass drum Boom-~~Crash~~ Boom - Crash
oh dear, he split the drum skin and inside
he found a tiny door mouse, he ran up Ben's
trousers and bit him on the ~~bott~~ bottom.
Now a big spot light shines on the
sawdust arena - and Tara-! on comes
the ring-master Captain Custard - ~~oh~~
~~how~~ he wears a red coat the same
colour as ~~his nose~~ daddys nose, a
big black top hat, white trousers and blue
riding boots, all the children clap him
clap clap clapity clap, all except one little girl 173

THE GREAT BIM-BOM CIRCUS

Everybody at the Bim-Bom Childrens Circus was very excited, they were going to perform at London Towns famous Hampstead Heath - the seats were full of children who were full of jelly babies, suddenly the Bim-Bom Band struck up under it's conductor Fred Nose, Omm pah-pah went the Tuba played by Dick Twit, Tootley Toot went Doris Cabbage on the Flute, she blew so hard the elastic in her knickers broke and they fell down - then Ben Barmy the drummer hit his bass drum, Boom Boom - Crash Oh dear! he split the drum skin and inside he found a tiny door-mouse, he ran up Ben's trousers and bit him on the bottom.

Now a big spot light shines on the sawdust arena and Ta-ra on comes the ring-master, Captain Custard he wears a red coat the same colour as daddys nose, a big black top hat, white trousers and blue riding boots, all the children clap him, clap clap clapity clap, all except one little girl called Rosemary she clapped when she had an ice cream in one hand and it all splashed out and went in a little boys ear hole.

Captain Custard cracked his long whip and it caught him on the back of his neck, he let out a yell and his hat fell over his eyes - "Ladies and Children Bim-Bom Circus proudly presents, Crimple the Crown-the - Oh I'm sorry, I meant Pimple the Clown".

called Rosemary she clapped when she had an ice cream in one hand ~~ad~~ and it all splashed out and went in a little boys ear hole.
Captain Custard cracked his long whip, and it caught him on the back of his neck he let out a yell. and his hat fell over his eyes - "Ladies + Children Bim-Bom Circus proudly presents ~~Pimple the~~ Crimple the Crown - the - oh Im sorry I meant Pimple the Clown - Taa-raa - went the band and Pimle came on - he did 20 Summer saults and 10. Winter ones - he did a hand stand 100 → a foot stand and an impression of a hat stand in a funny voice he said How do you do - do do you how - then like magic he took 10. Big Sun flowers out of his trousers and he balanced them on his head, his nose, his knee - then he walked off on his hands - Then Tarara - Captain Custard cracked his whip and caught him self on the bumm! Ow! he went, and his eyes watered - "Now" he said "we have the mighty Pakistani Curry muscles"! Oh! on came a very strong man - very very strong - he even smelt strong 203

Taa-raa - went the band and Pimple came on, he did twenty summer saults and ten winter ones, he did a hand stand, a foot stand an an impression of a hat stand. In a funny voice he said, "How do you do - do do you how" - then like magic he took ten big sun flowers out of his trousers and he balanced them on his head, his nose, his knee then he walked off on his hands - Then, tar-ara - Captain Custard cracked his whip and caught himself on the bumm! Ow! he went and his eyes watered.

'Now' he said "We have the mighty Pakistani Currymuscles" Oh! on came a very strong man - very very strong - he even smelt strong. He showed his huge muscles and the children clapped, and a little boy got more ice cream in his ear hole. Mr. Currymuscles said "Ladies and Children I now break world Guinness Book record, I swallow 100 pounds of Mars bars", and in one gulp they were gone - you could hear them going down into his belly - rustle, rustle they went because he forgot to take the wrappers off! "Ladies and Children" he announced "I feel sick". Then he bent down and grabbed two big purple dumb bells, (they could'nt speak) "I now lift up 10 million tons" with a big strain, his knees knocking, his eyes crossed, he lifted the 10 million tons up and split his trousers 'Ha ha ha' laughed the children.

He showed his huge muscles and the children clapped, and a little boy got more ice cream in his earhole, Mr Currymuscle said "Ladies and Children - I now break wored Guiness Book record, I swallow 100 pounds of Mars bars, and in one gulp they were gone - you could hear them going down into his belly - rustle-rustle they went because he ~~forgot~~ to take the wrappers of. "Ladies and Children" he announced "I feel sick" - then he bent down and grabbed ~~a~~ big purple ~~weights~~ dumb bells (they couldn't speak "I now lift up 10 million tons", with 100→ big strain he knees knocking, his eyes crossed, he lifted the ~~weight~~ 10 million tons up and split his trousers, "Ha Ha Ha" laughed the children - then a spot light went on the top of the tent and it showed a tight rope - and waiting to go on was a clown in a red suit with white bobbles on - "A big hand for Willy Wibble ~~Wobbe~~ Wobble" so some one gave ~~Captain Custard~~ a ~~big hand~~ Willy ~~Wobble~~ Wibble Wobble 171

Then a spot light went on the top of the tent and showed a tight rope, and waiting to go on was a clown in a red suit with white bobbles on. "A big hand for Willy Wibble-Wobble," so someone gave Willy Wibble Wobble a big hand, but he already had two, so he put it in his pocket, then got on his blue wheel and whizzed across the wire and back the children clapped, more ice cream in the little boys ear.

Now while the circus was going on - outside in a tent was a real gypsy called Vera Fatlegs, who could tell your fortune - a little boy called Tom Lumps went in, the gypsy told him his fortune, it came to 30p, well she charged him 30p so Tom Lumps went away with no fortune at all.

~~bu~~ a big hand, but he alreaday had two so he put it in his pocket, then he got on his blue ~~whel~~ wheel and whizzed across the wire and back — the Children clapped, more ice cream in the little bap ear Now while the circus was going-on — outside in a tent was a real gypsy lady called Vera Fatlegs who could tell your fortune — a little boy call. Tom lumps went in. the gypsy told him his fortune. it came to 30P, well she charged him 30P so. ~~he went~~ Tom lumps went away with no fortune at all. 100

Back in the Bim Bom Circus Captain Custard had caught his neck a crack again as he announced 'Ladiessiss + Childrennnn — a very dangerous act - all the way from Wistambul we have Smelly Sam from Turkey — the band played some Turkish delight music and came Smelly Sam with his head a bandaged up on the NHS, he had a long mustache that finished behind his head, he had ~~five~~ five long sticks of liquorice with fire on the end he poked the fire in his mouth and screamed then he swallowed the fire ~~ate the liquorice~~ ate the liquorice and went 198 ~~home~~ for a drink of water

Back in the Bim-Bom Circus Captain Custard had caught his neck a crack again as he announced 'Ladiessiss and Childrennnn a very dangerous act - all the way from Wistambul - we have Smelly Sam from Turkey' - the band played some Turkish delight music and on came Smelly Sam with his head bandaged up on the NHS, he had a long moustache that finished behind his head, he had five long sticks of liquorice with fire on the end, he poked the fire in his mouth and screamed, then he swallowed the fire, ate the liquorice and went for a drink of water. The children all clapped alot clap + 10,000 they went. Now all the lights went out and a big spot light showed a little Elephant called Trinkle Trunk - and on his back was a clown in blue, his hame was Tinkle Tonk, the elephant raised his trunk and went 'Whoo whee woo' and ran round and round the ring while Tinkle Tonk juggled with coloured oranges, as Trinkle Trunk ran around, the children laughed as his bottom wobbled like a jelly, then Trinkle Trunk stood on his back legs, Tinkle Tonk went on juggling but fell off "You naughty naughty naughty naughty elephant". But the elephant just dipped his trunk in a bucket of water and squirted it all over him - then there was a little interval and girls went around selling ice cream to the children, all except one little boy who had enough in his ear.

The children all clapped a lot. clap + 19000
they went, now all the lights went out
and a big spot light showed a little
Elephant call Trinkle-Trunk - and on his back
was a clown in blue his name was Tinkle. tonk
the elephant raised his trunk and went "Whee whoo
Whee Woo" and ran round and round the ring
while Tinkle-tonk juggled with coloured oranges
as ~~the~~ Trinkle Trunk ran around the children
laughed as his bottom wobbled like a jelly
then ~~&~~ Trinkle Trunk stood on his ~~fro~~ back
legs, Tinkle Tonk went on juggling but fell off.
"You naughty naughty naughty naughty
elephant" But the elephant just dipped his
trunk in a bucket of water - and squirted
it all over him - then there was a
little interval and girls went around
selling ice creams to the children all except
one little boy who had enough in his ear.
Then Tarabang crash roar - "ladies +
Children the last act is Golden Growl
the lion and his trainer Tinkle Tonk again -
There was a great roar a Golden Growl
leaped into the ring and showed his teeth

Then, Ta-ra bang crash roar - 'Ladies and Children the last act is Golden Growl the lion and his trainer, Tinkle Tonk again', there was a great roar as Golden Growl leaped into the ring and showed his teeth, Tinkle Tonk showed his teeth but on one clapped. Tinkle Tonk made Golden Growl leap in the air and twist his tail - then 'Oh dear!' Tinkle Tonk put his head in Golden Growl's mouth then he could'nt get it out - then Golden Growl sneezed and Tinkle Tonks head fell, he made Golden Growl promise never to do it again - then he said "Give a savage growl for the children", 'GROWWELLLLLL' went Golden Growl but it made him feel giddy and he had to sit down.

Then there was a great roll on the drum, and the drummer ate it.
'Ladies and Children', said Captain Custard, 'for the grand finale here are all the turns' - and on came Pimple the Clown, Currymuscles, Willy Wibble Wobble, Smelly Sam, Vera Fatlegs, Trinkle Trunk, Golden Growl, and Tinkle Tonk, they all stood on each others shoulders and sang God Save the Queen, and the children all went home happy.

Tinkle Tonk showed his teeth but no one clapped.
Tinkle Tonk made Golden Growl leap in the
air and twist his tail - then oh dear -
Tinkle Tonk put his head in Golden Growls
mouth then he couedint get it out -
the Golden Growl sneezed an Tinkle Tonks
head fell, he made Golden Growl promise
never to do it again - then he said "Give
a savage growl for the children
GROWWLLLLL went Golden Growl
but it made him feel giddy and he had
to sit down - Then there was a great ~~foo~~
roll on the drum· and the drummer ate it.
"Ladies and Children said ~~sopp~~ Captain
Custard - for the grand finale here are
all the turns - and on came Pimple the
Clown, Currymuscles, Willy Wibble Wobble
Smelly Sam, Vera Fat legs, Trinkle Trunk
Golden Growl + Tinkle Tonk, they all stood on
each others shoulders and sang God Save
the Queen, and the Children all went home
happy.

The End

December 1954: Camden Theatre. A *Goon Show* rehearsal. Back row: Wallace Greenslade, Harry Secombe. Front row: Peter Eton (producer), Spike, good-looking Eric Sykes..

Nod the Snail

Once upon a time there was a mummy snail and a daddy snail, they lived in some rocks in the corner of the garden, and they came out at night to eat some vegatable leaves, they were very ordinary snails and like all snails moved very very slowly, but then they had a baby snail, and he was called Nod, he was a very ordinary snail too and grew up to be just as slow as his mother and father, until one day, there were some men working in the garden, they were mending an electric wire, and one night Snod was crawling over the wire when suddenly "FLASHHHHHH.. WHOOSHHHHHH? he touched the live electric part and Nod shone like an electric light bulb, and suddenly he started to move about so fast, he zoomed around the garden like a motor scooter, when the people from the house went into their garden next morn -ing, they saw this snail go whosssshhhhh, past them ,then whossh back again, then whoosh up to the top of the tree and the whoossh down again, he was going so fast no one could see what it was, so they got a net and put it in the garden , sure enough suddenly whoosh Snod came rushing by and whoosh!, he went right thru the net!. so next they dug a hole in the garden and along came Nod, and whoosh! he went right over the whole to the other side and dissappeared across a field, so they called the Police, the family said "Look theres something very small and fast that rushes thru our garden, it frightens all the cats and dogs and chickens and all the old grannies whose knickers fell down! Nod went so fast he whizzed up the Motorway at a hundred miles an hour, he past everything, some people who were driving their cars suddenly all shouted, "Help! look! theres a snail going past us at a hundred miles an hour! so they told the police and the =police gave chase in very fast motor-cars and with a special box they caught Nod, imagine their suprise when they saw that Nod was a snail, "The policeman said " Gh dear, its only a little snail, how can he go so fast! " Soon Nod was very famous,because he was the fastest snail in the world, so he got his picture in the newspapers, and he even went on television, and he was on (NAME OF CURRENT CHILDRENS TV SHOWS),Now over in America they have world champion snail races, and the winnder gets a Gold cup and 50p, so they entered him for the rase, and they took him by Concorde Jet plane, in a little box. In the race were ten other champion snails, and came the great day , they were all lined up ready for the race,the starter said" Ready- steady go"! and off went the snails, but then whoshhhhhhhh,and ~~NOdx~~ Nod shot over the finish line,no one could believe it, all the other snails were still right at the start! and he went to meet President Regan the Boss of America, then ~~other ends~~, so Nod ~~xxxxx~~ won 50p and a Gold cup,/the Police took him back to England and he went on Television with Terry Wogan,and he was on the News, but really Nod wanted to be back in his garden with his mum and dad, so he stopped going fast, and moved very slow like other snails, every body was very worried about him, they took him to a snail doctor who said "Theres nothing wrong with Nod, all snails move slow like him" But they said "He used to go very fast" and the snail doctor said "Well thats when he must have been sick, because snails don't go fast," so now hes going slow means hes better". So the police took him back to his garden and let hi -m go, and there he met his mum and dad again, and they were so happy to see him, because they thought he was dead, and they took him home and they had a lovely snails dinner of lettuce leaf and chips.

The story is written to include, counting,textures,descriptions,moral justice, sentoment,family togetherness. Nota Bene: Certain words are underlined, and in reading they should be stressed to give emotional bite to the story.

T H E - S Q U I R R E L - F A M I L Y ·

Once upon a time there lived a lovely Red squirrel called Charles,he had a beautiful warm red furry coat,and a big bushy tail big and red like teachers nose, Charles was married to a lovely lady squirrel called Lady Di,they lived in a Oak Tree, and this tree was nearly three hundred years old, it was so big, it would take twenty children holding hands to go round it. Charles and Lady Di had found a lovely big hole high up the top of the tree, to make their home in, and sometimes Charles would sing a song and he and Lady Di would do break dancing, sometimes they would break a chair sometimes a table .Charles loved Lady Di very much and one day Lady Di told Charles she was going to have a baby and he fain -ted and went BONK! on the ground, so Lady Di poured a bucket of cold water over him and he felt much better. Together they made a little bed of nice clean dry grass and they put daisy flowers all the way around for when the baby squirrel was born and Lady Di started to knit a pair of silly-socks for the baby ,because any squirrel wearing socks would look silly. Charles went off to collect plenty of nice fresh nuts so there would be plenty of food for when the baby arrived, Charles liked collecting nuts, most of his friends were nuts. One morning the baby was born, and when Lady Di told Charles he fainted again and BONKt on the floor,but after she threw a bucket of water over him he was much better. The baby squirrel was a boy, and they called him Little Willy. Little Willy was sooo little, just the size of your thumb. Lady Di ga -ve him lots of milk to drink, and Charles said "I think you're giving him too much cows milk" and Lady Di said"Why" and Charles said because he keeps going Moooo-Moooooooo"! Soon the Summer came and Charles took little Willy to teach him how to walk along the tree branch, and Charles fell off and went Bonk on the ground,so Lady Di threw a bucket of water over him and he felt much better. Soon little Willy was big enough to walk on the branches alone, but Lady Di had told him "Be very careful, that some big bird or a pussy cat does'nt catch you and eat you up", and, there was a big black crow called Rotten-Dicky-Bird/who tried to catch little Willy by the tail, but then brave daddy Charles came out and shouted "If you touch my little Willy again, I'll set fire to your tail feathers and burn your bottom"! ~~tree and you'll have boiled eggs in your nest~~", "Caw" said the crow because that was the only word he knew. Then one day Little Willy fell out of the tree and broke his leg, but! an old gardner, Tom Sillybom, saw poor little Willy and said "Oh dear" he picked poor little Willy up but OUCHHHHHHHH! Willy bit him on the finger, so, Tom had to put on anti-squirrel gloves and took Willy to the vets Mrs Funnyconk, she put little Willys leg in plaster and put him in a box near the fire, ~~poor little Willy was so sad. His poor mum and dad were looking every where for him shouting "Little Willy, where are you". LadyDi was crying and crying and crying~~ ~~[illegible]~~ ~~she made the floor all slippery~~ wet ~~and Charles slipped on it and went Bong on the ground~~. Tom Sillybom, the gardner and his wife looked after Little Willy very well, ~~but~~ and ~~son~~ soon/Little Willys ~~his~~ leg was better, and he started to leap all over the house, o-ne night, Mrs Sillybom got such a fright! because Little Willy had jumped into a bowl of Jelly and Custard, Mrs Sillymom shouted "Helllllp! theres a jelly and custard with legs running round the room! One Sunday morning, they let Little Willy out into ~~in~~ the garden and he ran straight across the lawn and up the Old Oak tree to his mum and dad, ~~and there was Lady Di pouring a bucket of water over Charles~~ and when they saw him Charles fainted and Willy ~~he~~ helped Lady Di pour a bucket of water over him to make him feel better, and they all lived happily ever after ~~until Childrens Television Time.~~

(S)

ARE YOU GOING TO GET AWAY WITH THIS

He laughed at my note and said, 'I always live in hope.'

A LIFE AFTER DEATH STORY FOR CHILDREN

Once upon a time there were two butterflies, with green, gold and red wings, they were called Mr. and Mrs. Lovely. One day Mrs. Lovely laid two little white butterfly eggs under a leaf, so the rain wouldn't give them a cold, after a few days the eggs hatched and out came two brown and yellow spotted hairy caterpillars, they looked round; one was called Ding, and the other was called Dong, when they stood together they were Ding-Dong. Ding said: "I'm so happy being a caterpillar".

"So am I" said Dong.

"We are both young, and we are going to have a lovely time eating nice green leaves, playing caterpillar games, and lying in the sun and sleeping in the moon". They had a super time, sometimes birds tried to eat them, but no! Ding and Dong looked all smellypoo - and the birds didn't want to. Ding and Dong used to eat a hundred leaves a day! They were very happy, but one day, they both started to feel very strange, they got all sleepy and they didn't feel happy anymore, their friend, a big black beetle called Tiggle Toggle said, "I think you are both going to die!".

"Oh dear" said Ding, "Oh Ding", said Dong. "What happens when we die" said Ding.

"Well" said the black beetle called Tiggle Toggle, "Some people say you go to heaven".

"What's heaven like?" said Ding and Dong.

"I don't know" said Tiggle Toggle. "people say it's a place where God lives and when you die you go there and he makes you happy".

"We don't want to die" said Ding and Dong. "We're already happy". Then a deep voice said "There's no such place as heaven".

They looked up and there was a big black vulture called Lumpy-conk. "When you die that's the end of you", he said and flapped his wings.

Poor Ding and Dong cried - the next week Ding and Dong fell asleep, and slowly they turned into dirty brown cocoons. They stopped moving and became very still. "Yes" they're dead said Lumpy-Conk. "I'm going to eat them all up". But Tiggle Toggle the beetle said "Don't you dare!"if you do I'll bang you on the beak with a conk-hammer.

This frightened off Lumpy-Conk who flew away to his nest to play his banjo.

All winter the two little cocoons of Ding and Dong lay still, stuck to the leaves and everybody said "Poor things, they haven't moved for over a year, they must be dead". and everybody forgot all about them except Tiggle Toggle the beetle, who came once a month and put little forget-me-not flowers by the bodies. But, one sunny day, Tiggle Toggle was walking along a branch to put flowers on Ding and Dong when he saw something magic happening!

The two little coffins of Ding and Dong split open .... and out came two beautiful butterflies, scarlet and green and purple.

"Whoopee" said Ding and Dong. "Look at us! We're not dead anymore" and they flew up and down the garden drinking honey from the flowers and playing æroplanes.

"Tiggle Toggle was right" said Ding. "This is better than being a hairy caterpillar".

Tiggle Toggle the beetle was right, there <u>is</u> a heaven, and they flew through the summer gardens with thousands and thousands of coloured flowers.

The Cat.

My wife to be ~~Tessa~~ Tessa Jones and I were standing at the altar about to be married – the vicar was about to say I now pronounce man and wife the Cat. A Black cat appeared at the altar. My instinct was to bend down and stroke it. But no, the moment I touched it, It snarled backed away and lashed at me with her claws, it drew a long red bloody scratch on my hand which started to bleed. It stood there and howled at me, until the priest drove it away. She said holding a crucifix, she is the devil. Balls! a cat is a cat. my on a voice trembling with fear. It's a cat. my scratches turned septic, they became serious. I was hospitalised, with a high temperature. I was given penicillin, penacillin-penacillin. It felled my arm was amputated. In 24 hours. guitar players. All on 24 hours. That bloody cat – It disappeared. The bloody thing leaving me with one arm – I carried a a small automatic pistol – if ever I saw that bloody cat !!!

28 Sept 99

201420

Sam

I'm here God.

Where are you

One night coming out of a Pub, I saw the cat, cast by a cars head lights. My God was I imaging it, he was a big as a large dog, in fact the size of a panther, I drew my pistol, but he was gone. In the following weeks – news paper spoke of the killing of sheep by a large animal, believed to be a panther that had escaped from the zoo, pot armed police patrols were looking for it. A month later, December, it was freezing. ~~There was a tap at~~ I was seated before a blazing log fire. Something drew my attention, my God it was the huge cat, it scratched at the window, it wanted to come in. I reached for my revolver, and opened the window, it came in very smoothly, cat like, and the lay in front of the fire, I sat there fascinated, there was a knock on the door, it was a policeman' we have followed the beast sir to here 'Yes' I said then awkwardly. 'Yes its asleep by the fire' Can I come in sir' he said cocking his pistol. Taking aim he shot

PTO

The beast it gave a piercing howl.
He became smaller and smaller – and
dissappeared. leaving only a blood stained
Carpet

Sent To S.M.

THE CAT by Spike Milligan 27-10-99

My wife to be Tessa Jones and I were standing at the altar about to be married - the vicar was about to say I now pronounce you man and wife when the Cat a black cat appeared at the altar. My My instinct was to bend down and stoke it but no, the moment I touched it it snarled backed away and lashed at me with his claws, it drew a long red bloody scratch on my hand which started to bleed it stood there and hissed at me until the priest drove it away holding a crucifix. "She is the devil" he said in a voice trembling with fear. Balls the cat isn't the devil it's a cat my scratch has turned septic they become serious. I was hospitalised with a high temperature I was given penicillin,penicillin,penicillin it felt my arm was complete me a guitar player. All in 24 hours that bloody cat it disappeared the bloody thing leaving me with one arm. I carried a small automatic pistol if ever I saw that bloody Cat!!!

One night coming out of a pub I saw the Cat cast by a cars headlights. My God was I imagining it he was as big as a large dog,in fact the size of a panther I drew my pistol but he was gone. In the following weeks newspapers spoke of the killing of sheep by a large animal believed to be a panther that had escaped from the zoo armed police patrols were looking for it. A month later,December,it was freezing I was seated before a blazing log fire something drew my attention my God it was the huge cat it scratched at the window it wanted to come in. I reached for my revolver and opened the window it came in very smartly, cat like, and the lay in front of the fire I sat there fascinated there was a knock on the door it was a policeman "We have followed the beast Sir to here" "Yes" I said then awkwardly "Yes it's over by the fire" "Can I come in Sir" he said cocking his pistol taking aim he shot the beast it gave a piercing howl then became smaller and smaller and disappeared leaving only a blood stained carpet.

DOLORES. TYPED THIS: ITS O.K.

VERY BAD JELLY

BAD JELLY WAS MENDING her broom stick watched by Devil, the evil black cat, who was playing with a dead mouse.

Oh, why don't you eat' said Bad Jelly.

'Im not hungry' moaned Devil.

Then give it to Horrid the Hairy dog.'

'Hes out hunting rabbits' said Devil. 'Hes trying to catch one for you to cook for dinner to night.

But Devil was old and could'nt catch a Rabbit so she went to the fishmongers a bought a fish.

Bad Jelly II ate the fish bones and all Help!

Ive got a fish bone in my throat' so they lowered willy the worm down with a hook to pull it out.

'Oh thank you willy it was very kind of you' and ate him up

Willy the worm in the witchs belly.

But Willy the worm found his way out the back. Where he was met by Grump the elf, who took to tea in a tree, but Gump gave Willy a magic mushroom and he turned into a crow But, the crow did'nt Caw but started meow.

Caw-meow-caw-meow, what next a crow cat?

Bad Jelly sat in her castle, watching a big cauldron coming to the boil 'Oh Im very hungry, I must go and get a boy or girl to eat

Jim and Rose were walking back from school thru the woods. 'Be careful said a friendly tree, theres a witch about, Just then Jim Rose were thrown in a sack by the witch

Tee-hee – cackled the witch. I'll have them for my supper and I'll give some to Devil my cat.

But Grump heard them calling Help that sounds like somebody in trouble, so he walked towards the sound of Help. Then he saw the sack with someone struggling to get out, so he got his Swiss Army knife, cut the string and out rolled Jim and Rose and a Duck!

'How did he get in' said Grump

'He was in here when we got on' The witch was going to eat him with us and chips' said Rose.

How many times did I say, 'Please, Spike, write me a follow-up to Bad Jelly'? Total lack of interest – until this arrived.

‘You must be hungry’ said Grump

‘Yes, we’re starving, we have’nt eaten for 3 days’ said Rose

‘Then you must force yourselves’ said Grump. He took Rose Jim and the duck to his strawroofed cottage on top of a mountain. Sit at the table’ he said

Then cooked them fried eggs and bacon an a big pot of tea Jim and Rose gobbled up the meal in 3 minutes.

‘My you must have been hungry’ said Grump ‘Now you can have a sleep in my bunk beds’

‘I’ll have the top bunk’ said Jim

‘No, you wont’ said Rose ‘I’ll have it’

‘Oh don’t argue over it’ said Grump, ‘Well toss for it heads or tails?’

‘Tails said Rose but it came down heads so Jim slept in the top bunk. But they could’nt sleep because an owl kept hooting all night. Jim clamped his beak together with a clothes peg.

The owl was so angry he flew down and bit Jim on the bum

‘Ow! My bum’ shouted Jim ‘Hes bitten my bum, but I can’t see where’.

Never mind said Rose I’ll put a plaster on it said Rose

But oh dear, the plaster came off in the bath ‘Don’t worry said Rose ‘I’ll kiss it better, so Rose kissed Jims bum better.

‘You are a very good girl, not many sisters would kiss their brothers bum.

Yes she was a very brave girl,’ said her mother ‘Im going to tell the Queen about it. So she told the Queen ‘Oh what a brave boy, bring him to the Palace’ So Jim was presented at court, and the Queen gave him the Victoria Cross for bravery

That afternoon Jim and Rose were climbing trees, when they came across a crows nest, it had three eggs which were about hatch, as they did out flew 3 witches on broomsticks flew out heading for the moon. On the moon was a witches convention they were all preparing terrible spells that they would put on children, they were all dancing and screaming round a huge bonfire on which they were burning models of boys and girls ‘Im going to eat three girls’ screams a witch and Im going to boil three boys for soup screamed another with. Then the all jumped on their broom sticks and flew to the earth each wicked witch looking for a boy or girl to eat. Jim and Rose were asleep in Grump’s cottage, Jim was dreaming of apple pie and Custard, Rose was dreaming of making dolls clothes. They were in bed because they had measles, Measles was an illness that witches were terrorfied of catching, as they flew in the window of Grumps cottage, they saw the measles a screamed with terror, but too late they caught measles and the measles caught them. The all had to go to a witchs measle hospital, so they would'nt fly away and spread it their broomsticks were all locked up

The witches started crying tears of acid, that burnt their clothes, making holes in them, so you could see in. They were crying for the return of their broomsticks, without them they could'nt fly anywhere and find boys and girls to eat 'I have'nt seen an witches for a while' said Jim

'No they must be tired' said Rose.

Witches dont get tired' said Jim, they run on batteries, they must be charging them.'

Yes, the witches broomsticks were battery charged with three speed gear Low - middle - fast, SUPER FAST, some witches broomsticks could do a 100 miles per hour, but they had to hold tight and put their seat belt on. If they exceed the speed limit the ZONE police would pull them over and fine the £50 for speeding. 'This is a violation of privacy' one screamed; who only had £49 pounds.

Jim and Robin were scrumping apples from a tree in the farmers field. They were delicious, very big a red a full of juice. They took some home to Grumpy and he made them into cider, it was very strong, and after drinking some Jim & Rose fell fast asleep. While they were in the land of Nod It snowed, and the whole countryside was blanketed in white. Using a sledge made by Grunge, the pulled each other around the field They found a hill, and that was it, they spent the whole day sledging down it. At the end of the day Grunges served them up with piping hot potatoe and Pea soup. That night they went to sleep by a roaring log fire. The world seem'd wonderful

It was Christmas week and it was snowing. Grung had a big sleigh pulled by two Reindeer. They went into Tinsel Town Christmas Shopping. Jim & Rose bought Grunge a pair of fleece lined slippers. On Christmas Eve they made a little Nativity scene, with baby Jesus in a straw cot. They heard someone singing carols at the front door they were Tree Goblins and their families with a lantern, Grunge gave them ten shillings, and they were so pleased the sang an extra Carol

Jesus bless this house

with its cat and mouse

They bought a Christmas from a Fairy Christmas shop, they did it all up with silver stars, little colored candles and shiny colored ball, then they wrapped all the presents in coloured paper, with big white labels, and waited for the day.

Christmas Eve, they all put their night clothes on sat around the fire and told Ghost stories. Then the cuckoo clock cuckooed nine, time for bed. As the night was cold Grung gave each of them a hot water bottle

They were so excited the could'nt sleep So Grunge gave them each a glass of hot mulled, and that sent them to sleep. While they were Grunge filled their stocking with little toys apples and nuts. It was such a happy morning Santa Claus had done his duty.

But Jim big present, was a big fort and a box of soldiers to (*original word is illegible*). It Rose had a lovely fairy doll, with three changes of costum They were so happy they hugged each other. Rose spent the day shampooing her dolls blonde hair. Jim spent the day getting his soldiers to capture the fort. It was a very happy. Suddenly in the fire place there was a blinding light, there sparkling bright was the Fairy Queen. 'Hello children, are you happy with the toys Santa brought you'?

'Oh yes, said the children, would you like to stay for a glass of wine'? Yes she would. She drank three glasses of wine and started to giggle. 'I better go before I get to tipsy' she said and vanished leaving behind a lovely smell of scent. So, with that ended the Children's Happy Christmas.

THE END

I was often asked whether I thought Spike was a genius. No, I didn't. But he had a great creative talent – a gift – in that he was able to sit down and write a poem or story with no hesitation. All in one go, as above.

B

But Willy the worm found his way out the back. When he was met by Grump the elf, who took to tea in a tree, but Grump gave Willy a magic mushroom and he turned into a crow But, the crow didn't Cawl but started meeow.

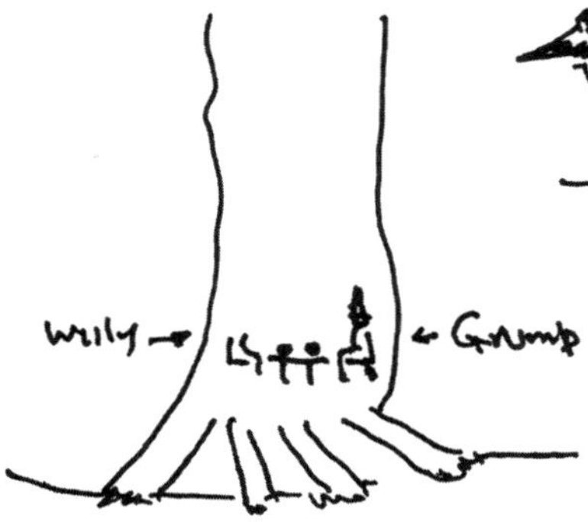

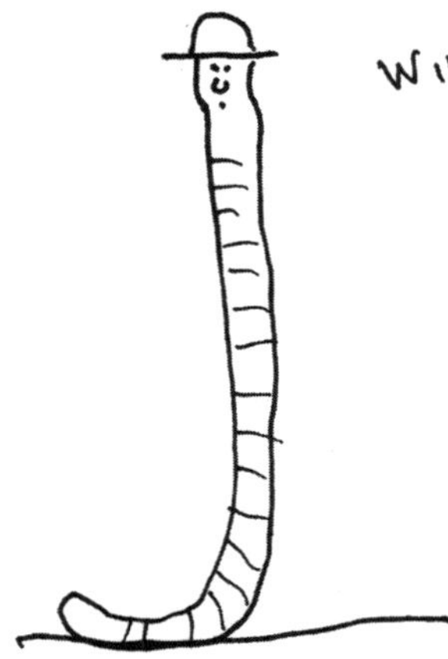

Willy the worm

Grump

Horrid

Caw-meow - Caw-meow, what next a crow-cat?

Bad Jelly sat in her castle, watching a big cauldron comin
to the boil 'Oh I'm very hungry, I must go and get a
boy or girl to eat. Jim and Rose were walking back back

from school thru the woods, 'Be careful
said a friendly tree, theres a ~~witch~~ witch
about, just then Jim & Rose were thrown
in a sack by the ~~witch~~ witch

Tee-hee- cackled the ~~witch~~ witch I'll have them for
my supper and I'll give some to Devil my cat.

But Grump heard them calling Help, thats sounds like somebody
in trouble, so he walked ~~towards~~ towards the sound of Help. Then he
saw the sack with someone struggling to get out, so he got his Swiss
Army knife, cut the string and out rolled Jim and Rose and a Duck!
'How did he get in' said Grump "He was in here when we got in'
The witch was going to eat him with us and chips' said Rose
"You must be hungry' said Grump' Yes we're starving. we
have'nt eaten for 3 days' said Rose "Then you must force yourselves'
said Grump. He took Rose Jim and the duck to his straw roofed
cottage on top of a mountain. Sit at the table' he said
Then cooked them fried eggs and bacon an a big
pot of tea, Jim and Rose gobbled up
the meal in 3 minutes. 'My you
must have been hungry'
said Grump "Now

you can have a sleep in my bunk beds" I'll
have the top bunk" said Jim "No you won't' cut
Rose 'I'll have it' 'Oh don't argue over it said
Grump 'We'll toss for it, heads or tails?' -Tails
said Rose' but it came down heads so Jim
slept in the top bunk. But they couldn't
sleep because an owl kept Hooting all
night. Jim clamped his beak to gether
with a clothes peg.

D

The owl was so angry he flew down and bit Jim on the bum
'Owl my bum' shouted Jim 'Its bitten my bum' but I can't see
where". Nevermind said Rose I'll put a plaster on it" said Rose
But oh dear! the plaster came off in the bath" Don't worry
said Rose, 'I'll kiss it better, so Rose kissed Jim bum better.
"You are a very good girl, not many sisters would kiss
their brothers bum. Yes she was a very brave
girl", said her mother" Im going to tell the Queen
about it. So she told the Queen" Oh what a brave boy,
bring him to the Palace" So Jim was presented at
court, and the Queen gave him the Victoria Cross
for bravery

That afternoon Jim and Rose were climbing trees,
when they came across a crows nest, it had three
eggs which were about hatch, as they did out flew
3 witches on broomsticks flew out heading for the
moon. On the moon was a witches convention
they were all preparing terrible spells that
they would put on children, they were all dancing
and screaming round a huge bonfire on
which they were burning models of boys and
girls 'Im going to eat three girls' scream a witch
and Im going to boil three boys for soup scream
another with. Then the all jumped on their
broom sticks and flew to the earth each
wicked witch lookin for a boy or girl to
eat. Jim and Rose were asleep in
Grumps cottage, Jim was dreaming of apple pie
and Custard, Rose was dreaming of making
dolls clothes. They were in bed because
they had measles, measles was on illness
that witches were terrorfied of so catching
catching, as they flew in the window
of Grumps cottages they saw the measles
a screamed with terror, but too late
they caught measles and the measles
caught them. The all had to go to
a witches measle hospital, so
they wouldn't fly away and spread
it their broomsticks were all
locked up

E

for ~~them to~~

The witches started crying tears of acid, that burnt their clothes, making holes in them, so you could see in. They were crying for the return of their broomsticks, without them they couldn't fly anywhere and find boys and girls to eat

'I haven't seen any witches for a while' said Jim 'No they must be tired' said Rose. Witches don't get tired' said Jim, They run on batteries, they must be charging them".

Yes, the witches broomsticks were battery charged with ~~the~~ three speed gear low-middle-fast 100 SUPER FAST, some witches broom sticks could do a 100 miles per hour, but they had to hold tight and put their seat belt on. If they exceed the speed limit the ZONE police would pull them over and fine them £50 for speeding. 'This is a violation of privacy" one screamed who only had £49 pounds.

Jim and Robin were scrumping apples from a tree in the farmers field. They 200 were delicious, very big a red a full of juice. They took some home to Grumpy and he made them into cider, it was ~~very~~ very strong, and after drinking some Jim & Rose fell fast asleep. While they were in the land of Nod It snowed, and the whole countryside was blanketed in white. Using a sledge made by Grunge, they pulled each other around the field They found a hill, and that was it, they spent the whole day sledging down it. At the end of the day Grunges served them up with piping hot potatoe and pea soup. That night they went to sleep by a roaring log fire the world seem'd wonderful

..

F

It was Christmas week and it was snowing. Grung had a big sleigh pulled by two Reindeer. They went into Tinsel Town Christmas Shopping. Jim & Rose bought ~~gra~~ Grunge a pair of fleece lined slippers. ~~Ev~~ On Christmas Eve they made a little Nativity ~~sce~~ scene, with baby Jesus in a straw cot. They heard some one singing Carols at the front door, they were Tree Goblins and their families with a lantern, Grunge ~~gav~~ gave them ten shillings, and they were so pleased they sang an extra Carol

Jesus bless this home
with its cat and mouse

They bought a ~~Christmas~~ from a Fairy Christmas shop, they did it all up with ~~S~~ silver stars, little colored candles and shiny colored ball, then they wrapped all the presents in coloored paper, with big white labels, and waited for the day.

Christmas Eve, they all put their night clothes on Then sat around the fire and told Ghost stories. Then the cuckoo clock cuckooed nine time time for bed. As the night was cold Grung gave each of them a hot water bottle

They were so excited the could'nt sleep So Grunge gave them each a glass of hot mulled, and that sent them to sleep. While they were Grunge filled their stocking with little toys apples and nuts. It was such a happy morning Santa Clause had done his duty.

G

But Jim big present, was a big fort and a box of soldiers to
man. It Rose had a lovely fairy doll, with three changes of costom
They were so happy they hugged each other. Rose spent the day
shampooing her dolls blonde hair. Jim spent the day getting his
soldiers to capture the fort. It was a very happy. Suddenly
in the fire place there was a blinding light, there sparkling bright
was the fairy Queen. "Hello children, are you happy with the
toys Santa brought you"? "Oh yes, said the children, Would you
like to stay for a glass of wine"? Yes she would. She drank
<u>three</u> glasses of wine and startted to giggle. "I better go before
I get to tipsy" she said and vanished leaving behind a
a lovely ~~scent~~ smell of scent. So, with that ended the
the Childrens Happy Christmas.

The End

1960: The last series of the *Goon Show*. Spike reading his final script.

1967: A *Bed Sitting Room* rehearsal.

A MILLIGAN MISCELLANY

. . .

The BBC have asked me to write a hundred and fifty words to go along with this cassette. Fish, love cupboard ripe, leg, pencil, house, nail, teeth, kiss, flute, elephant giant, honey, rabbit, scouse, lamp, whistle, cup, clarionet horse, grain, Poona, rust, gutter, plimsole, hurt, dental client, musket, plinth, calf, mutton, if, no, but, fish nun, broom, ball, cliff, age, Kenneth, cob, slur, angle pin, dent, plinth, dog, ease, ear, lentil, nose, grey, desert, lino, glint, earth, chal, hair, dirt, porridge, note court, cannon, live, ant, garment, spook, cannon, diet, coke, oil, bustard, gannet, net, spice, lemon. guitar, string. dote, dont, minute, sterile, saint ranger, moon, coat, nether, lint, stamp, hand, oats noon, kitten, earth, tea, party, lemon, lute, gong priest nonsense pickle brain, curve, rick, nest, dog easy fox. bolt, second, honk, doubt, curtain lid ache, axle, dolt, pun, liver, tin, milk, oboe, pink, ton wheel, buck, norman. dive, trap, trot, poke, pig pound, lentil, soup, trundle, trap, ink, wad, tick, flute, note* telegraph, cart, bullock, pack, forage, cut, tin, lid, egg, seam, torrent, roger, vault, item, itch.

Spike Milligan

* used twice for effect

I asked Spike to 'write 150 words' as an intro for a BBC cassette. This is what he sent me.

Quasi Modo. I can tell
That name that name
With the help at The rings a bell
the hard.
Hes in the tower at Notre D.
He rings the bell where ever Stafford he am
Hes such a ugly bugger
With a ~~Hes got~~ an umpty back

Quasi Modo

Quasi Modo I can tell
That name rings a bell
~~He rings the bell where ever~~
He ~~rings the bell where~~
Hes rings it in the Notre Dame
He rings it where ever he am
Esmarald was the love of Quasi
He was not good looking was he?

This is a perfect example of Box 18: scraps of paper and his reworking of Quasimodo. They were published in *A Mad Medley of Milligan* – but I thought it was so typical.

The Leshic Lakit Lee
Will be the death of me
& The leshic lakit Lee
Is very hard to see
It attacks your head
Will your laying in bed
~~Does the leshic lakit lee.~~
But I foiled the leshic lakit Lee
By staying awake you see!

Lesic Lokit Lee

The Lesic Lokit Lee
Will be the death of me
The Lesic Lokit Lee
Is very hard to see
It attacks your head
When your laying in bed
I foiled the Lesic Lokit Lee
By staying awake you see!

Babu

Babu Babu
Indian Banker
People say hes just a wanker
~~H~~ He's says, no I'm not
Look at the ~~mon~~ money I've got
So they looked at the money he ~~g~~ got
And,
That was his lot.

Sea

I was walking by the sea
When it splashed me.
People with wet trousers
Are not welcome in peoples houses.
They might ~~even~~ laugh at me
But I'll blame it on the sea
See?

Being you - whats it like just being you
Just the thought of seeing you
Blows my mind away.
And your face
Like a fire in outer space
All the grace and the pace
Of the hundred meters
Hunting Cheethas
What to do
When you meet somebody who
Puts some kind of spell on you
Goes and rings the bell on you
Its hell on you
So then you just stand and wait
Like a beggar at the Palace gate
Hoping for that burning Satyr glance
A smile perchance.
The voice that sets your heart a-dance
I wish I knew
Just what its like.
Being you.

Monte
Written Feb 4.87

S Milligan
Mar. 88.

DATE: 30th August, 1990 TIME: 4-50 p.m.

ATTENTION: H.R.H. THE PRINCE OF WALES

COMPANY:

FACSIMILE NO:

FROM: SPIKE MILLIGAN

NUMBER OF PAGES (including front page): 2

IF YOU DO NOT RECEIVE ALL PAGES PLEASE ADVISE US IMMEDIATELY

9 ORME COURT, BAYSWATER, LONDON W2 4RL, ENGLAND.

Spike Milligan

Twas in the year of 1990 A.D.
That Prince Charles was struck down by a tragedy
Polo was his favourite game
And that is the fiend sport to blame
When taking a swing at the ball
He did to the ground fast fall
Landing there on his right arm
Which the fall did cause him to harm
He had broken a bone in two places
And could no longer put on his own braces
Worst he could not play the fiend Polo
Which made his spirits sink so low
And while living in one of their houses
Di had to help him on with his trousers
He was writing with his left hand
And not a word could anyone understand
So he booked into the N.H.S.
To try and ease his financial distress
And all the nation did pray
That his right elbow would be O.K.
And so we all hope with hand on heart
That his arm will not come apart
That the operation will be a success
And reported in the Daily Express

WILLIAM McGONAGALL.

Spike and Peter Sellers loved William McGonagall. They used to send each other poems in his style. Spike sent this to Prince Charles when Charles broke his elbow playing polo.

There was a time when Bondi Beach was a swimmers and surfers paradise - then came a day when a new pennant was raised, it was called "The Shit Flag" it meant the current was bringing sewage ashore - it took Europe 2000 years to reach that level of pollution - it took Australia just two hundred.
I first saw Australia in 1958, I'd say I caught it at a stage just before the critical change that took place in the ensuing 30 years which all but wiped out the old Australia culminating in the winning of the America Cup and the Bi-centenial - whether it was for better or worse is a matter of opinion. In the immediate post-war years, in the eyes of the western world, Australia was backwater, it rarely appeared in or on the news save when there was an England-Australia Test Match - will you bear in mind, at the time, Australia, a country the size of the U.S.A. had a population of 5,000,000, by no means was it a commercial giant, but no one was starving, the people still talked of England of 'Home' or 'Old Dart', the feeling that Queen Victoria was not quite dead still pervaded the older generations, thinking in modern terms, bearing in mind Chinas unsolved dilemma of 1,000 million people - I'd say Australias 5,000,000 was just about right - with the population stabalising at that figure, the country's as yet unexploited mineral wealth would be held in trust for future generations of Australia. At that time my mother, an ordinary working class person bore out my opinions when she wrote in 1953 "This wonderful land of sunshine and plenty" - don't forget, the word 'plenty'. There were of course those who thought selling Australian resources was good business. This was all right with renewable resources, wool, butter, lamb, but it was the selling of expendable minerals - iron, coal, destruction of rain forest for wood chip etc, that will cause a short fall for future generations, maybe 2-300 years, but it would come. I will use my home town - Woy Woy as a microcosm of change during those 30 years. In 1950, Woy Woy dreamed on the Brisbane Waters, there was space, there was quiet, the journey by steam train from Sydney took (change at Hornsby) 2½ hours, a journey through the magnificent Kurangi Chase. Individual compartments with buttoned upholstery, water jugs, foot warmers, at Hawkesbury a man patrolled the platform selling "Hawkesbury Oysters, Shilling a Jar". When you steamed into Woy Woy - there'd be a coal fire in the waiting room, a meat pie and floater stall on the platform. Ron Widow and his taxi would usually be waiting (if not you'd have a beer at the Railway Tavern). You'd

squeeze in and Ron would drop you off one by one, yarning all the way "Mrs. Tinkers 'avin an operation fer her veins". At home in Orange Grove Road, the night would be welcomed by possoms in the white gum behind the house - there were green tree frogs and blue tongued lizards - on the waters black swans. In the middle was St. Huberts Island - across the ripe up Daleys point were the pecked carvings of the extinct Dharug tribe - in that quiet I wrote my first best seller. It's all gone no more black swans, increased population, more motor boats, water skis, electric open plan trains, sealed green glazed windows, from 6.00 a.m. 'till 9.30 a.m. the commuter lunatics roar past my mother's home, the tree is empty of possoms - green frogs - the last blue tongue killed by domestic dogs. St. Huberts Island built over by Hookers - even my appeal to Lady Hooker received no reply - but then the population was now 15,000,000 as some people say "we're <u>only</u> 15,000,000 - a long time ago someone said that in China, and so the Woy Woy I knew perished under population pressure, or as some say progress. I remember in 1953 an estate agent pointing at the green hills around Brisbane Waters and saying "One day they'll all be covered in houses" - he was right - now what?

I see barbaric sodium city lamps
pretending they can see.
They make a new mad darkness.
Beyond their orange pools
  the black endlessness of time beckons,
What, in that unseen dark tomorrow
  is waiting.......
That iron tomorrow, coming on
  unknown wheels
Who is the driver,
Will he see me in time?

Woy-Woy
NSW
Oct. 1971

September 1972. The poem at the end of this was later included in *Small Dreams of a Scorpion.*

Crush hot-

·lips that feel for some others, and smothers.

Khol black-

eyes irradeing abduction, seduction.

Smoke from a Gitane, in mid light

~~Bells~~. ~~from~~ a church telling mid-night

Bells;

And the scent of that par-fume lingers

Ikons.

black face virgins ~~adoring~~ adorning,

([redacted])

Jade - is the light from the rue gasolaire

Is there some one out there

knows about this affair

Who can handle a

Scandalé in Bohemia.

Spike Milligan.

July 8 1990

for Duncan Lamonte

Norma Dear

My Car is down the SIDE OF THE SYNAGOGUE — CAN YOU FEED METER.

ALICE, BLOODY AWFUL

Love

Me

Premiere night of *Alice in Wonderland*. He played the Griffin. Obviously he didn't think much of it.

Bronte Parsonage

It seem'd I went there in a dream. I was on tour with a variety show. I chose a dark Sunday evening, in winter, a cold rain was falling when I approached the door of the Bronte Parsonage, there on a polished brass plate was the words The Reverend Patrick Bronte. There were no tourist about, when I pulled the ~~bell~~ door bell, I heard a tinkling in the hall, there was a rattling of keys ~~then the great dark Oak door, and open~~ a rattling of bolts, and there stood the care taker, Good-evening sir, my name is Spike Milligan, the name he knew, I said I knew it was late and a Sunday and raining, but I ~~choose~~ especially chose such an evening to visit the Parsonage, I knew well the story of the Brontes, would he allow me a visit of the building, he smiled and said 'Of course Spike' come in. I felt comforted at him using my first name. In the parlour was ~~chaise~~ long on it had died Emily Bronte. In Charlottes bed room was her bed made up as if ready for the night, a cold wind was shaking the shutters, that very sound Charlotte must have heard. The most remarkable room was one in which as children they had drawn in pencil, the lower wall was full of them - it was haunting - child haunting.

Now Anne, fearing death was near, wrote a poem poignantly expressed, it began

A dreadful darkness closes in
On my bewilded mind
Oh let me not suffer, and not sin
Be tortured yet resigned.

I ~~too saw the bed in which she died.~~ ~~Then Branwell's room very simple~~ in it he had died ~~from drink and drugs. The Reverend Brontes family were passing away~~

In an attempt to revive her, the family sent her to an Hotel in Scarborough, Charlotte accompanied her, alas Anne died in one of the hotels rooms. Her grave is in the town. The the disease affected Charlotte, before the illness took hold she married Mr Nicholls, alas not long after Charlotte died. I shall never forget my visit to the Bronte Parsonage

Norma, included this in Vol 1 of my life story

WHAT LIFE STORY.

spike milligan

9, Orme Court,
London, W.2.

19th December, 1969

John Hyman, Esq.,

~~Dear John,~~ My dear John,

Take two of these before retiring, and then one three times a day; morning, lunch and early evening. They may make you feel thirsty, and give you a dry mouth, so keep a glass of water by the bed. Two days on these can't hurt you; might give you a little breathing space.

I have been on them four years, and they manage to keep me going. They are not addictive.

Let me know how you feel in a couple of days time. (Christ, I sound like the family doctor!)

Love, Light and Peace,

Spike

Spike

The caring Spike, when my husband (now ex) was ill.

Early Poetry -

Where are you now
My beautiful love
Where oh where are you now

Does another posess you
Do other eyes distress you
And do you in the night
Think of me
Of me and that Sunny day
When we were young
And dreams came true
Those dreams that have gone
Gone - leaving only the dust of
a once great flame -

This was originally written hastily in pencil
in 1951 - to Toni Pontani

Dec 1 1980 Frustration

My mind is overflowing
but its nowhere to go

N here with castle + dragon

No 6/10 Could Do Better
Talk to me.

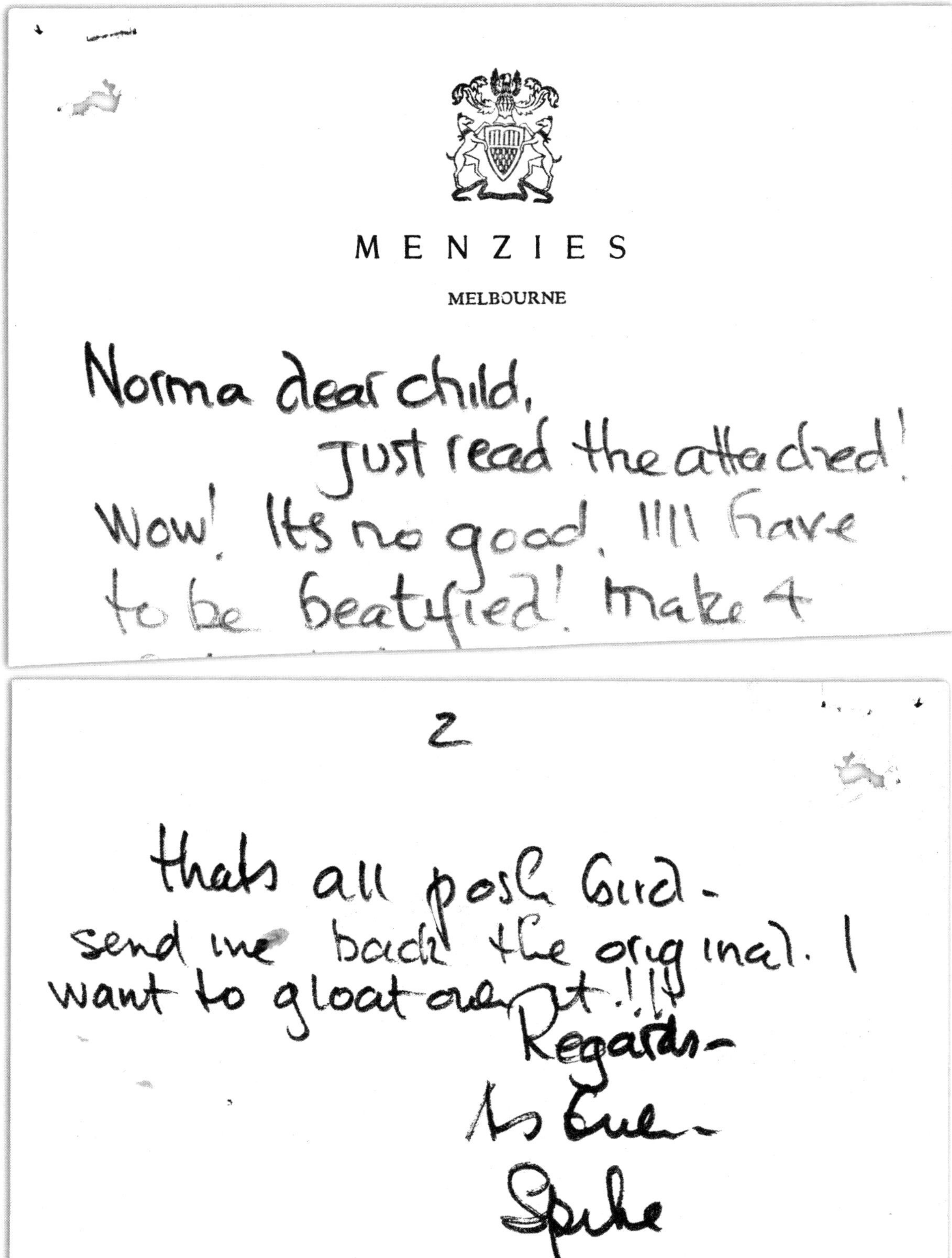
MENZIES

MELBOURNE

Norma dear child,

Just read the attached!

Wow! Its no good. I'll have

to be beatified! make 4

2

thats all posh Gud -

send me back the original. I

want to gloat over it!!!

Regards -

As Ever -

Spike

Spike happy with a write-up for once.

0442-230627

One central point of fire and ice
A thousand moons melt down
There is a luminous
dimand in my mind
The sharp edges tear the brain
Central a cobra sees to strike
please god can he do it soon

Ho park

Waiting - we are all waiting -
waiting for the waiting to stop

Please God.

Please some one.

Let me light my candle.

Somewhere, somehow, A God
was trying to tie in a knot in
us, and we let him. A bird of
Paradise was flying. but with
different hues, we must have
been blind not to see him

Tabetha my furry dove

" ' " Love

So How this family all were smitten

When you are here as a kitten

Now you have gone to Valhalla ~~afar~~

Killed By a speeding motor car

~~By a speed~~

I saw you

At Moondazzle

~~And you were there~~

Roll right stones

In the dark

In the rain

The bird of night

empty of song

Gondarland together again

there are no frontiers

We together again

this awful penalty

for living, called

Death -

How dare they bear me

Into such horror -

With no warning

I see the dawn light

touch the swans neck

And a temporary life

is born

The summer was in our hands
We lay like fallen apples
in the grass, and as
we lay intertwined, it seemed
we, ~~like the sky~~, were endless
~~until that first dusk~~
~~dove down kiss, I thought~~
~~lips were~~, we were drowning
in each other, yet neither
called ~~for~~ help, somehow we
had reached Camelot, the
stars came out and blessed
us, we could hear the sea
we searched each other and
found ourselves, call it love yet
it was better than that, we
made each other happen, ~~it~~
~~was one second, that's all~~

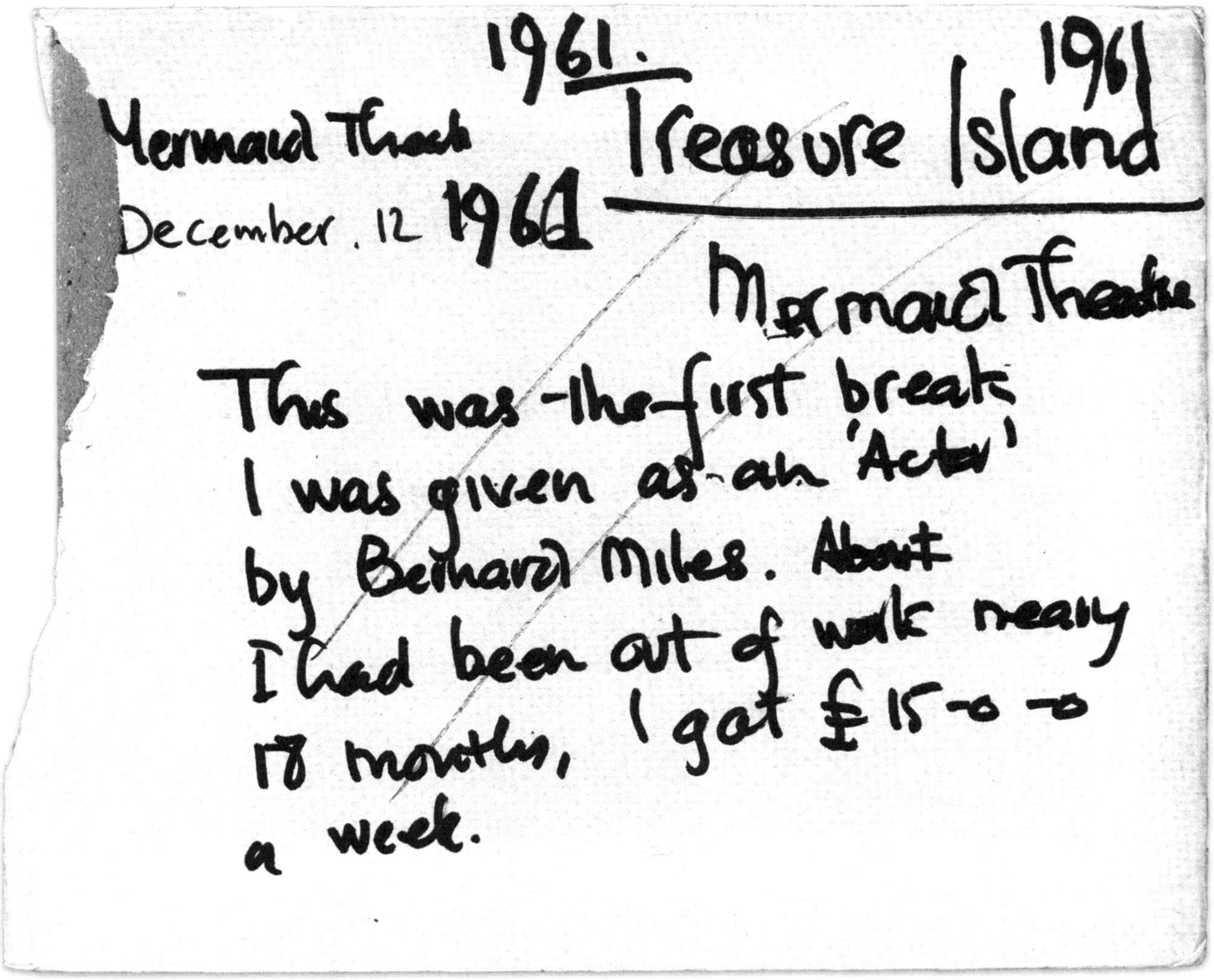

This envelope contained the first photographs taken of Spike in the role of Ben Gunn (opposite). He was indebted to Bernard Miles all his life. I once asked Spike, 'When does the debt get paid?' His answer: 'Never.'

Ben Gunn, Mermaid Theatre.

Spike with his 'best mate'.

g.5
3
7.5
cm
NO BRICKS

2.
7.5
cm
deep
NO
BRICKS

TREE MANIAC

(1)

The Tree Maniac.

Announcer: Good evening, the BBC Home Service presents the Grunes (pause) Grunes? Grunes??? yes it quiet definately written here G-R-U-N-E-S, of course they must mean Coons - yes thats it - Coons (walks away repeating)

John Snagge (Peter) Mr Greenslade is currently being treated by Sir Charles Fees the famous Phychaitrist and used car salesman. What Greenslade meant to say was that This is the Grute Show (Pause) Grute?, now they mean Grune - h + G the Grune Show

[Long Silence]

Oboe Gives hurried tuning A to Orchestra

Snagge Bai Jove I do believe they werent quite ready - Have another try Ladies and -

Orchestra Come in too soon with signature tune.

[Pause]

FX Fork falls on floor

This *Goon Show* was never performed. It was found by Spike amongst some of his papers after the *Goon Show* had ended. It appeared in a book in 1987 but not in Spike's own handwriting – thought you'd like to see it.

(2)

Ned Seagoon: That thrilling sound of a EPNS fork hitting the ground signals the start of a mysterious mystery.

Spike (starter) On your marks - get set -

FX Starters pistol.

FX Mass of boots running away

Ned Very well I do it on my own -

L+G. The Landing Tree Manual

ORK Brooding - mystery chords mixed with maniacal laughter + tree chopping.

Dimbelby The Queen places the ~~sap~~ Royal sapling in the Royal hole and with a silver shovel fills it in.

The Queen (Peter) I name this tree Copper Beech God bless its nuts and all who will assail her.

FX Feeble clapping.

Ann: Meantime - at Catford police station. a constable Oaf is at work

~~FX Truncheon hitting head.~~

Constable ~~(Spike cockney)~~ (beating a rubber bust of Mick Jagger.

③

Fx Truncheon on head

Constable. (Spike. Cockney) Take that you hippy swine

Fx. Truncheon wallop!

Constable! earnin' on that money

Fx Wallop

Constable singing crappy tunes!

Fx Wallop!

Constable and me with my fine voice only on 18 quids a week

Fx Wallop

Fx Phone rings.

Constable Hello - Hello - better pick it up but first

Fx Wallop

Fx Picks phone up

Constable Catford Police station.

Neddy: ~~Hello~~ this is Neddy Seagoon. Welsh midget. and Forester in waiting to the Queen!

Constable Oh, you ever seen that swine Mick Jagger - he gets £200,000,000 a minute

Fx Wallop

Neddy Yes - I want to report -

Constable: and me only £18 a week-
FX Wallop
Neddy: Listen constabule of old Catford.
I wish to report a tree vandal-
Constable Oh - is ~~that~~ it a doggie?
Neddy Is what a doggie.
Constable (Barks) Bow-wow-wow-woof-Grrr-
~~thats a d~~
Neddy Whats that?
Constable Thats a doggie!
Neddy I thought you were a policeman
Constable I am and its only £18 a week
FX Wallop
Neddy Look- you know Hernes mighty oak
in Windsor Park?
Constable Well not personally..
Neddy. Well its -
Constable - and he's always havin' it orf with
good lookin' birds-
FX Wallop
Neddy Look man! Hernes mighty oak has
been uprooted - roots and all
Constable - and 'ee's not even good lookin'!
FX Wallop (continues)

The *Harry Secombe Show.* Spike wrote on the back of this photograph: ' Must be the last get together of the Goons.' But there is no date. They appeared together in 1972 for the last *Goon Show* of all at

the Camden Theatre. I think Spike got it wrong; this looks to me like a *Goon Show* rehearsal or recording.

This is just Spike doodling for future ideas.

S/S
5
9

Ann: The BBC would like to point that what they are hearing. is not typical of the police force - the Inspector has said he personally is not jealous of Mick Jagger - its that bastard Paul McCartney.

Neddy: Its true - the £18 a week police were not interested folks - so I would have to go to the £10 a week police even 9 or 8! nine and eight make £17, that would only be a pound cheaper than the £18 a week understand (gibbers on)

Ann: Mr Seagoon is also being treated by Sir Charles Fees.

Neddy: - so money is no object - I'll just throw this shilling on the pavement to see if theres any Scotsmen in the district.

~~FX [illegible]~~

FX: Shilling on pavement. follow by approach of two sets of boots at speed - they halt

Grytpype-thynne: (breathless) M'card!

Neddy: Mac Hard - ah - a real scot! - see. Thynne Moriarty financiers - and 24 hour dry cleaners.

Moriarty:. Owww

Neddy The sound came from a shivering wreck wearing a wedding-tackle length vest. a topless bowler - ~~and~~ and a reconditioned cricketers box - laying stretched on the pavement

Thynne My partner. Count Jim 'Knackered' Moriarty a scion of Grade 3 Salmon has played the lead in several French post-cards.

Neddy: Is he dead?

Thynne That is a trade secret - but his strength is unbounded - with him we can cracked this case open.

Neddy So saying he cracked a case open -

FX Case being smashed. - brilliant

Thynne Thats just a beginning - you want Herons mighty oak traced

Neddy Yes yes yes yes yes yes

Thynne One yes would have done - you're used to working with the deaf or the Irish: Moriarty cover me with a song.

Moriarty (sings!) These teeth are the teeth of a woman in love (continued)

Thynne Neddy - So far our ~~enquiries~~ investigations have led us to this blank cheque - ~~[illegible]~~ it would help our enquiries - if you signed just here

FX Hurried signing

Thynne What a beautiful hand -

Mor Yes - but a terrible signature

These images were in his mind when he created the written words for the *Goon Show*

e told me, 'This is how I saw them when I was writing.'

(7)

~~Thynne~~

Thynne: – Moriarty, open the Cyprus Sherry.

FX Pop. and pouring.

Neddy: It, it looks like water – ~~it tastes lit~~

Thynne A toast to your forthcoming overdraft.

~~Neddy It tastes like water~~

FX Clinking glasses.

Neddy It – it tastes like water

Thynne Water? Theres and Old Latin adage Parventum – ad Hoc – nil desparandum Aqua frescha!

Neddy Oh – I wish I'd met you earlier.

Thynne So do we Neddy – say so do we for me Moriarty

Mor So do we!

FX Terrible slap.

Ow – mon tete!

Mor Why do you keep hitting him

Neddy Why? because hes <u>there</u>!

Thynne

Ann: Who would want to remove Herns Oak The first clue came from a couple living in Neasden.

FX Clock ticking – bed springs – ~~alarm~~ snoring. Alarm clock rings

Crun + Bannister. Waking noises

Crun Ah

Bannister Ooooo

8

~~Crun A~~

Bannister ~~Wake~~ Are you awake Henry'

Crun I'll just look in the mirror -
---- oh - is it open eyes for awake

Bannister Well thats how I do it!

Crun Whats the time

Bannister I set the alarm for 8

Crun Why theres only 2 of us

Bannister There must be 6 more some where -

FX Bong of Po.

Crun Oh -

Bannister Its very dark this morning - look how dark it is out

~~Crun~~

Crun Thats the blinds Min

FX Sound of door knob - and bolts ~~gen~~ being with drawn.

Crun (off mike) Oh min - there's something on the landing.

Min It must be the cat -

Crun No a cat could'nt do this - some ones left an Oak tree on the landing - cat's can't do Oak trees

Min Let me see - oh theres a label on it - From the Tree Maniac -

Crun I dont remember ordering a tree from a maniac.

9

Min It must be a joke

Crun No min - its not a joke - its definately a tree - Jokes don't have leaves on.

Min No ~~got~~ some jokes have whiskers on.

Both talk at cross purposes (fade)

Fx Heavy snoring.

Ann The snoring you hear is that of the duty fireman at Lewisham

Fx Phone ring. Snorer wakes up

Fireman (SPIKE) ~~(Spike)~~ Hello Lewisham fire brigade.

Crun Hello - we have a Tree on our landing.

Fireman Thanks fer telling me.

Crun Don't go - we want help

Fireman Well is the tree on fire?

Crun No

Fireman - We'll we can't come unless its on fire

Crun Min he says he can't come unless the tree is on fire

Min Oh I'll get a box of matches

Crun If you come now - we'll have it going by the time you arrive

Fireman Its very nice of you to put work my way

This is where I stopped

1974: The real love of his life.

1975: With Twiggy at a demonstration in Harrods against the sale of furs.

1958: Wine tasting at the Rheingold Cellar, Sydney. Spike always said he was an oenophile. Here he is trying to prove it.

SPIKE'S LETTERS

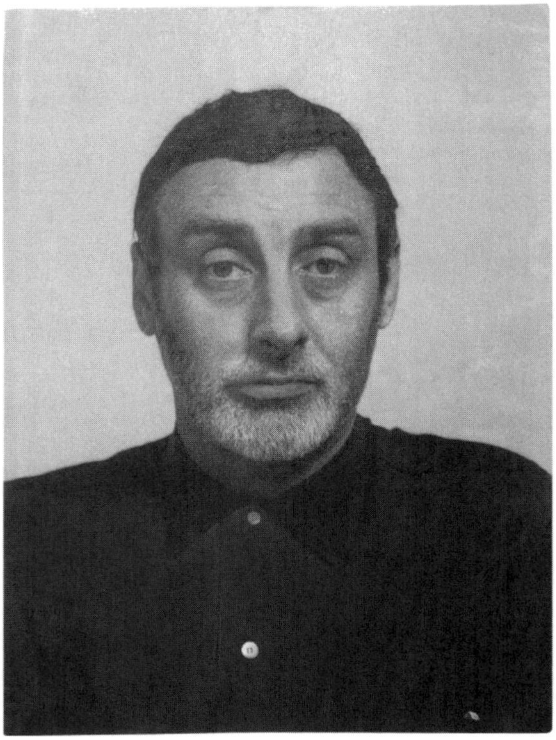

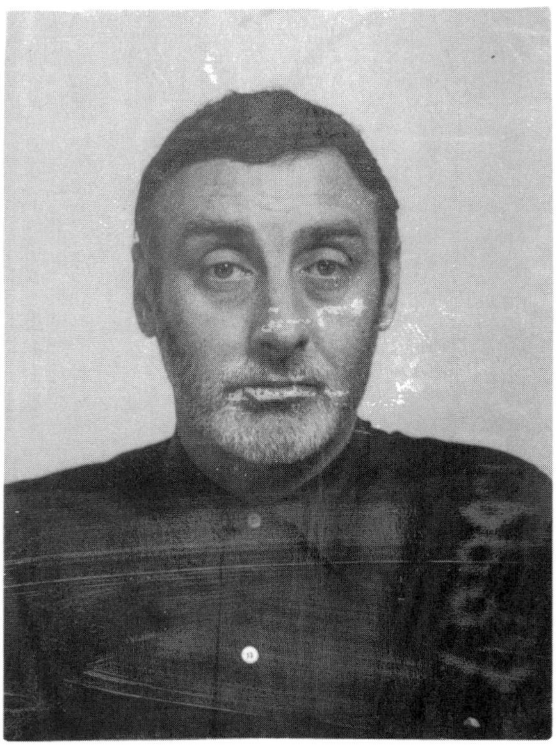

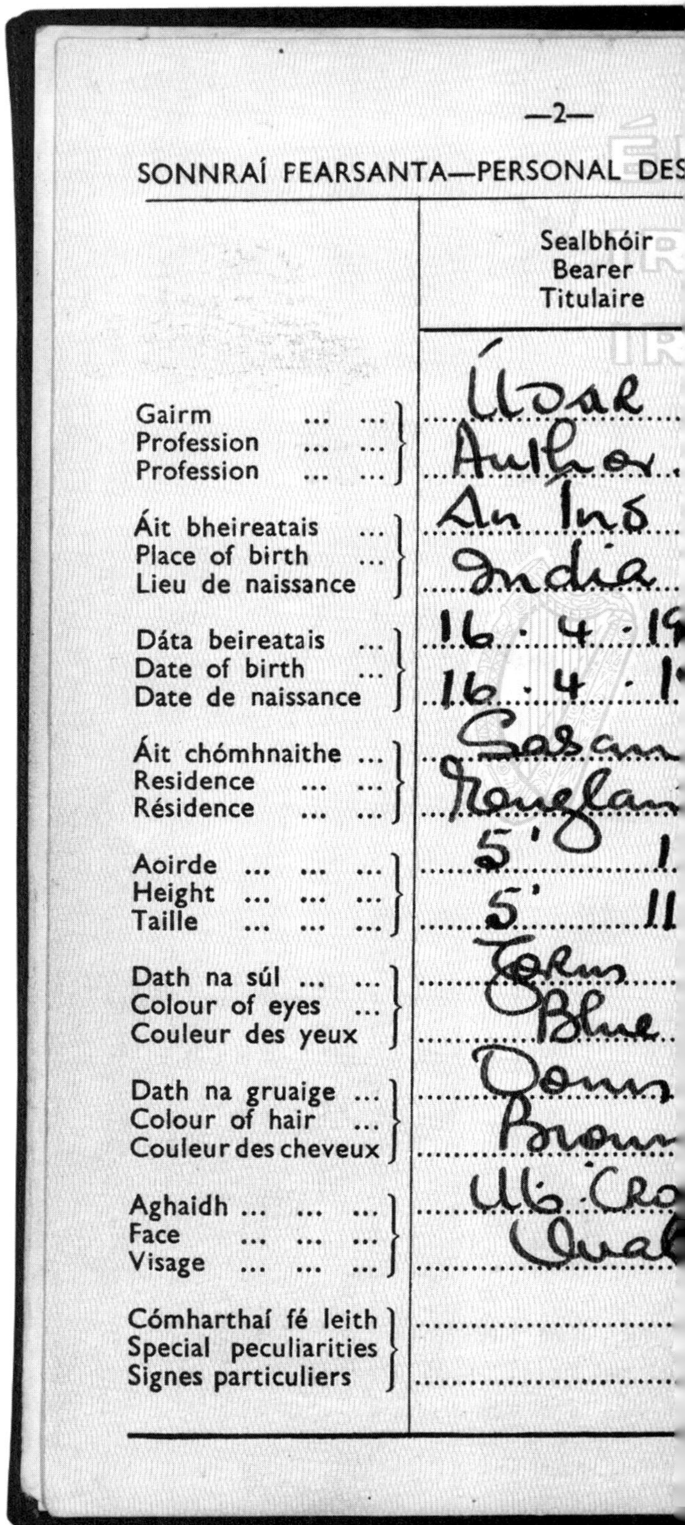

—2—

SONNRAÍ FEARSANTA—PERSONAL DES

	Sealbhóir Bearer Titulaire
Gairm Profession Profession	Údar Author
Áit bheireatais Place of birth Lieu de naissance	An Ind India
Dáta beireatais Date of birth Date de naissance	16. 4. 19 16. 4. 1
Áit chómhnaithe Residence Résidence	Sasan England
Aoirde Height Taille	5' 1 5' 11
Dath na súl Colour of eyes Couleur des yeux	Gorm Blue
Dath na gruaige Colour of hair Couleur des cheveux	Donn Brown
Aghaidh Face Visage	Ub Cro Oval
Cómharthaí fé leith Special peculiarities Signes particuliers	

Above: The passport photo he had taken for his new Irish citizen passport!

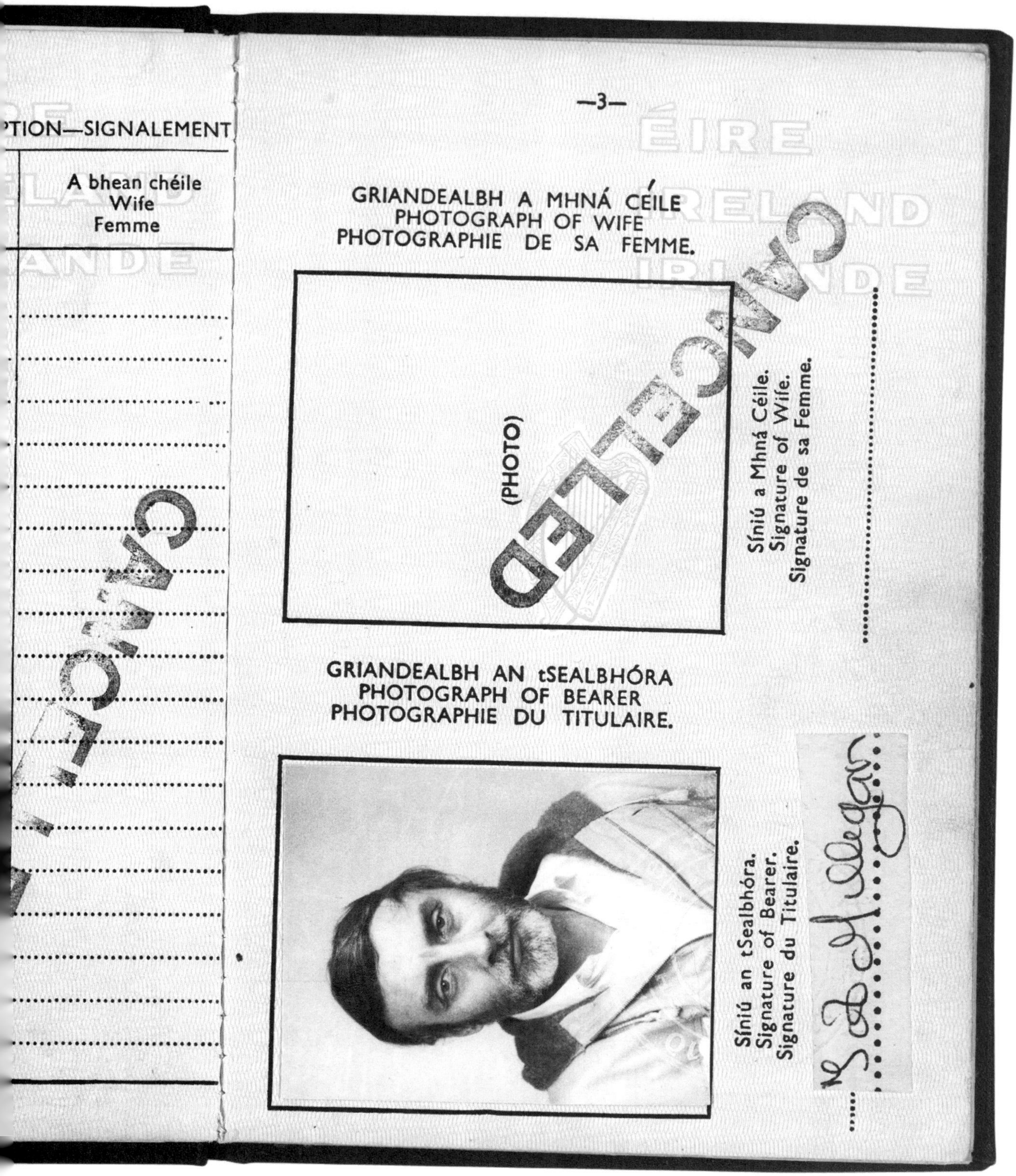

The true version of Spike becoming a 'stateless person'. Evidence of non-stateless person.

Spike's parents on their way back to Australia from the Himalayas.

TO OPEN SLIT HERE FIRST

BY AIR MAIL PAR AVION

AEROGRAMME

Hot Air Ballooning

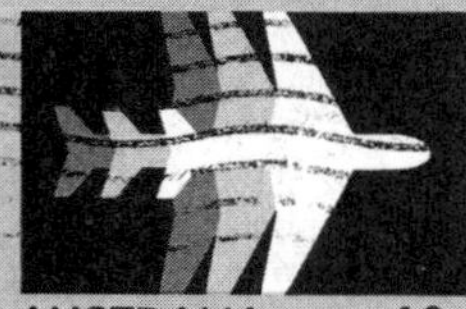

AUSTRALIA 40c

WOY WOY 4 30PM 20 AP 1984 N.S.W.

To

TO Miss. Norma Farnes.
9 Orme Court.
Bayswater
London W2.

COUNTRY OF DESTINATION England.

S.A.9. England.

From

SENDER'S NAME AND ADDRESS
Mrs. F. Milligan
393 Orange Grove Rd.
Woy Woy N.S.W.
Australia.

Postcode 2256.

FOLD SIDE FLAPS FIRST

FOLD SIDE FLAPS FIRST

Fold flaps before moistening gum. For maximum adhesion, press down for a few seconds. If anything is enclosed or any tape or sticker attached,

my photo was in the newspaper
behind the Flag Bearer & with the
Aussie Diggers. I know he will love
that. I've quite forgotten to ask you
"How are you Norma & Jack"? I do
hope all well. I keep pretty good
dear. Spike tells me he is coming
out end of June? is that right so
I don't suppose I shall see England
this year. Lets see anyway. Des Nadia
Michael & Mum all send their love.

[for your nice letter by by.] affectionately Grandma

My Dearest Norma.

XXXXXX

Love to Tanis mum & Jack

You must be thinking I've forgotten all about you. My dear you know I could never do that you are my adopted daughter, but I have had a lot of official functions thrust on me for the last six weeks or so.

You know Spike was doing the promotion commercial for our lovely new Shopping Complex in my city. & the Lord Mayor of Gosford City roped me in to carry out the opening ceremony & cut the Ribbon to open the "Complex. 30,000 people flocked through the doors as soon as it opened. I was feted and photos taken with the Mayor directors of the stores (45 shops) inside. all top class. I am just getting ready the photos etc. to send to my dear Spike. I have been very worried. (don't tell him this) about his eyes. Are they really getting better Norma. It is awful when one is so far away. I know I could not do much if I was there.

By the way, I march in the Anzac annual march with the digger's & my air force girl pals we all meet every year. I wear dad's medals and away I go. I am sending Spike that photo as well as soon as I get it.

How did the wedding go??

My dearest Norma,

You must be thinking I've forgotten all about you. My dear you know I could never do that you are my adopted daughter, but I have had a lot of official functions thrust on me for the last six weeks or so.

You know Spike was doing the promotion commercial for our lovely new Shopping Complex in Woy Woy. & the Lord Mayor of Gosford City roped me in to carry out the opening ceremony and cut the Ribbon to open the Complex. 30,000 people flocked through the doors as soon as it opened. I was feted and photos taken with the Mayor, and Directors of the stores (45 shops) inside, all top class. I am just getting ready the photos etc to send to my dear Spike. I have been very worried (don't tell him tho' about his eyes. Are they really getting better Norma. It is awful when one is so far away. I know I could not do much if I was there By the way, I went in the ANZAC annual march with the diggers & my Air Force girl pals We all meet every year. I wear dads 7 medals and away I go. I am sending Spike that photo as well as soon as I get it. My photo was in the newspaper behind the Flag Bearer & with the Aussie Diggers. I know he will love that. Ive quite forgotten to ask you How are you mum and Jack? I do hope all well. I keep pretty good dear. Spike tells me he is coming out end of June? is that right so I dont suppose I shall see England this year. Lets see anyway. Des Nadia Michael & Mum all send their love.

I'll write sooner darling. Thanks for your nice letter by by. Affectionately

Grandma

XXXXXX

How did the wedding go??

Love to Tanis Mum & Jack.

Now you know where Spike got it from: a truly formidable woman whom I loved.

Spike performing in *Idiots' Weekly* for ABC Sydney.

BY APPOINTMENT TO HER MAJESTY THE QUEEN SUPPLIERS OF CHINA, GLASS AND FANCY GOODS

HARRODS

HARRODS LTD
KNIGHTSBRIDGE
LONDON SW1
Telephone: SLOane 1234

BY APPOINTMENT SUPPLIERS OF CHINA, GLASS AND FANCY GOODS TO H.M. QUEEN ELIZABETH THE QUEEN MOTHER

SPIKE MILLIGAN ESQ.
9 ORME COURT.
LONDON W 2.

YOUR PERSONAL ACCOUNT NUMBER

4527326
19/12/65

PAYMENTS AND CREDITS MADE AFTER THIS DATE WILL BE SHOWN ON THE NEXT STATEMENT.

YOU MAY PAY YOUR ACCOUNT THROUGH ANY BANK BY USING THE CREDIT TRANSFER OVERLEAF. IF PAYING DIRECT, PLEASE RETURN THE TOP PART OF THIS STATEMENT.

RECEIPTS FOR CHEQUES WILL BE SENT ON REQUEST ONLY.

Cash £50/0/0. 6/1/66

DETACH HERE

DATE	DESCRIPTION	PURCHASES	CASH & CREDITS	REF. No.	FOR YOUR OWN NOTES
	BALANCE FROM NOV	406. 7.1			
8 DEC	CASH		50. 0.0	028	

AMOUNT TO BE PAID	AMOUNT IN CREDIT
356. 7.1	

HARRODS
HARRODS LTD.
KNIGHTSBRIDGE
LONDON SW1
Telephone: SLOane 1234

Spike's logic: Harrods took two years to do the job; he will take two years to pay.

BY APPOINTMENT TO HER MAJESTY THE QUEEN SUPPLIERS OF CHINA, GLASS AND FANCY GOODS

HARRODS

HARRODS LTD

KNIGHTSBRIDGE

LONDON SW1

BY APPOINTMENT SUPPLIERS OF CHINA, GLASS AND FANCY GOODS TO H. M. QUEEN ELIZABETH THE QUEEN MOTHER

Telephone Sloane 1234 Telegrams "Harrods London"

24 Jan 66

3

Miss Alice Bolton
Secretary to
Spike Milligan Esq
9 Orme Court
W.2

Dear Madam

re Spike Milligan Account

We enclose a further statement of account compiled to the 19th December from which after allowing your payment of £50.0.0d received on the 6th January, leaves an outstanding balance of £306.7.1d.

As stated in our letter of the 16th December, our terms of credit are for full settlement of accounts as rendered. We are therefore unable to agree to accept settlement of the enclosed account by instalments of £50.0.0d.

The Company's Annual Audit falls due on the 31st January and we must ask for a cheque in full settlement before that date.

Yours faithfully
Harrods Ltd

H T Dugdale
Accounts Dept

Ref: 4527326/48

9 Orme Court,
London, W.2.

26th January 1966

SM/AJB

the Chairman,
Harrods Ltd.,
Knightsbridge,
London, S.W.1.

Dear Sir,

I am being badgered into paying the enclosed bill. I decided to pay this bill at the same rate at which Harrods did the job, overall it took two years from the first phone call until the final completion of the job during which time I spent no less than 24 of my working hours attending workmen on the site who had come with insufficient instructions and also left all their paraphernalia in the front garden after the job was finished.

No I will pay this bill in the way I think fit and if you wish to take me to court I have a complete analysis of the work and I will be only too glad to let the press know how the work was done.

Yours faithfully,

SPIKE MILLIGAN

c.c. Louis Tarlo*

* His solicitor.

BY APPOINTMENT
TO HER MAJESTY THE QUEEN
SUPPLIERS OF CHINA, GLASS
AND FANCY GOODS

HARRODS

HARRODS LTD

KNIGHTSBRIDGE
LONDON SW1

BY APPOINTMENT
SUPPLIERS OF CHINA, GLASS
AND FANCY GOODS TO
H.M. QUEEN ELIZABETH THE QUEEN MOTHER

RHH/FEM

Telephone Sloane 1234 Telegrams "Everything Harrods London"

28th January, 1966

S. Milligan Esq.,
9, Orme Court,
London W.2.

Dear Sir,

I beg to acknowledge your letter of 26th January, 1966, on behalf of the Chairman, and in his absence from this office to-day your letter has been passed to the Managing Director for his personal attention.

Yours faithfully,

Robert H Hobart

Cdr. Sir Robert Hobart, Bt. R.N.
Personal Assistant to The Lord Fraser
of Allander

File >

HARRODS

HARRODS LTD

KNIGHTSBRIDGE
LONDON SW1

BY APPOINTMENT TO HER MAJESTY THE QUEEN SUPPLIERS OF CHINA, GLASS AND FANCY GOODS

BY APPOINTMENT SUPPLIERS OF CHINA, GLASS AND FANCY GOODS TO H.M. QUEEN ELIZABETH THE QUEEN MOTHER

Telephone Sloane 1234 Telegrams "Everything Harrods London"

Your ref: SM/AJB

17th February, 1966

S. Milligan, Esq.,
9 Orme Court,
London, W.2.

Dear Sir,

I have been asked by the Managing Director to investigate the complaints contained in your letter of the 26th January and in consequence I have seen Mr. Valentine the Manager of our Building and Decorating Department and obtained his report.

I am told the facts are as follows:-

Date of enquiry 10th March 1965
A representative called on the 19th March 1965
Our estimate FL.224 is dated 30th March 1965
Order was issued on the 3rd April 1965
The last entry in cost book regarding labour is week ending 15th August 1965

It would therefore appear that the job covered a period of about 4½ months including additional work to estimate. I understand the small amount of plant required for the work was stacked in the front garden and removed in early July when no longer needed. It would seem that the work was completed in a very much shorter period than as stated in your letter and I am afraid we are not prepared to accept settlement of your account by instalments and I trust that after further consideration you will be good enough to let us have your cheque in settlement without further delay.

Yours faithfully,

L. Stuart

L. STUART
Credit Manager

LS/CB
45 273 26

9 Orme Court,
London, W.2.

18th February 1966.

SM/SC/AJB

Mr. L. Stewart,
Credit Manager,
Harrods Ltd.,
Knightsbridge,
London, S.W.3.

Dear Sir,

The facts that you quote are the only facts you have. If you want to hear the real facts, take me to court, I would love to unfold the story very much, because I have really had a bellyful of the customer always being wrong. So go ahead, I'll see you in court.

Yours faithfully,

BY APPOINTMENT
TO HER MAJESTY THE QUEEN
SUPPLIERS OF CHINA, GLASS
AND FANCY GOODS

HARRODS

HARRODS LTD

KNIGHTSBRIDGE
LONDON SW1

BY APPOINTMENT
SUPPLIERS OF CHINA, GLASS
AND FANCY GOODS TO
H. M. QUEEN ELIZABETH THE QUEEN MOTHER

Telephone Sloane 1234 Telegrams " Harrods London Telex "

30 Mar 66

S Milligan Esq
9 Orme Court
W.2

Dear Sir

Thank you for your recent payment of £50.0.0d on account.

However, as stated in our letter of the 17th February, we are not prepared to accept settlement of your account by instalments and we must ask you, therefore, to let us have, by return, your cheque for £264.13.1d, as shown on the enclosed statement, to clear the balance still outstanding.

Failing receipt of your cheque, we will be reluctantly compelled to pass the matter to the Company's Solicitors for their attention.

Yours faithfully
Harrods Ltd

H J Dugdale

H J Dugdale
Accounts Dept

Ref: 4527326/48

9 Orme Court,
London, W.2.

31st March 1966.

Your Ref. 4527326/48

Our Ref. SM/AJB

H.J. Dugdale Esq.,
Accounts Department,
Harrods Ltd.,
Knightsbridge,
London, S.W.1.

Dear Sir,

By all means then pass it to your Company solicitors for their attention, I will instruct my solicitor likewise. I will look forward to this clash with utter and complete joy. I think my revelations will enlighten both you and the public in Court.

Yours faithfully,

9 Orme Court,
LONDON. W. 2.

Tel. PAR. 2768.

2nd June, 1967

The London Nameplate Manufacturing Co. Ltd.,
Zylo Works,
BRIGHTON, 7.

For the attention of:- Mr. Oliver.

Dear Mr. Oliver,

Further to our telephone conversation of yesterday afternoon, I should like to confirm that I require one brass plate, with the wording as follows:-

IN MEMORY OF A TULIP RALLY BADGE WON BY
BILL WARD, AND STOLEN BY SPIKE MILLIGAN
WHO WAS SUDDENLY TAKEN DRUNK.
MAY GOD HAVE MERCY ON HIS SOUL.

I should be grateful if you could make the plate with a small hole in each corner for screws, (enclosed is a sample).

I should like the same size as the previous two you have made for us 5" x 2½".

If you have any problems, please don't hesitate to get in touch with me.

I should be grateful if you could let me know when I could expect delivery.

Sincerely,

Norma Farnes
Assistant to Spike Milligan.

His saving grace was his conscience – never more so than here.

393 Orange Grove Road
Woy Woy
N.S.W.

Fridgy 27 Sept. 1968.

Hello Darling clever posh bird,

Sorry I have'nt written you a letter of any length, but life out here is getting bloody hectic, I'm now getting mail to answer and have no secretary, i.e. I've been up since 8, and as yet I have'nt started work on any thing I want to do , its all fan letters. letters from charities, from people who say ' You remember me I met you in 1934 etc etc', I have to sign forms for any work I do and post them all my self, this means a journey of 2 miles to Woy Woy Post office , I have to cut out write ups, read the papers to find out whats going on in the world. answer the phone, its now 12 O'clock, and I'm still answerijg letters. Nothing to report that desperately urgent, I'm doing occassional work to earn money , so far its reached the astronomical sum of about £,1000, for about two months, I'm trying to avoid drawing money from England because since devaluation the rate of exchange is unfavourable, I think I will be able to return the £1,000 to Coutts untouched, it was just a standby im case I bought a piece of land (I'm still looking). I did a Job for Channel 7 in Melbourne 'A Guy called Athol' its a show with one of thr original Seekers (They've disbanded) , I got them to pay for my mother to xomexaxzx go as well, we went on the Souther Aurora, a luxury air conditioned train, with a bar, Dining room, and a sleeping berth which folds into a comfy arm chair, built in are wash basin tpilet etc. Did the show, saw interest points, Captain Cooks Cottage, (Transported from England) , Cottage (later used as the State of Victori -as first Goverment House) of Charles La Trobe, first Govenor General of of Victoria, it was prefabricated in England and transported to Australia in 1839. (Did you get the envelope of flower petals from our garden? Hope so.) On the return journey we came back in daylight, and saw the countless rolling acres of sheep farms, passed the Famous Glen Rowan Hotel where Ned Kelly and his gang(Rebel Irish Hooray!) fought their last battle with the State Troopers. Bill Kerr will tell you all about it, talking of him '(The bloody thief, I learned that the act he used to do 'I've only got four minutes' was stolen from an old Australian comic, and thats why he did'nt ever c ome back to Australia, he is a scoundrel. We got home last night at about 10.30 at night, mum was whacked, it was good to get back to the clean air of the country and sea.

As always, telling me how hard he's working and the promise of his poetry book being finished (twice), to keep me quiet.

September 1977: Me in front of all the files. The missing files would be the ones he was working on.

So I'm back at the 'desk' writing, always bloody writing. Will you send the enclosed newscutting to Bill Kerr. Tell him I've been thru Wagga Wagga, and they say they're waitinf for him to get back half their bloody homes from him , tell him I met the small man from Warren Laytona and Sparks who sent Bill regards. Let me know how much my Mrs has sunk me for in money, just so I know. Don't forget to check with my letter about the odds and ends I want the painters to observe when finishing, i.e. seeing that all the sash windows are free and eased to allow them to be moved up and down . When they sand the floor, ask them to use a vacum sander, its one th t sucks up the dirt as it sands, after they've sanded, get Dorothy to 'Feather dust the walls to clean off any deposits, you may not be able to see them but they are there. Sorry you're bored, I feel helpless at the moment, all I can do is to try and finish the book before I return. I have decided that it will have to be a Trilogy, Part One From Joining the Army to going Overseas. 2) From going into action to the end of the War. 3) from the end of th4 War to Demob. Each book being thirty thousand words. I think thats what I'll do. I think. No more news. When I return I'll start writing the TV Show, I'd like it to be good. Phone Carol Jonas at Ronnie Scotts, tell her I love her and I think of her.(Must keep my birds happy) I don't know what to think about the Broadway 'Oblomov' I don't seem to be able to get excited about it, that might be a good thing. Give my love to our Posh Switch Board girl Kathy, tell her I love her . Have you got rid of all the surplus GPO Phones if not do so, also check all the other numerous GPO Lines that go up the back stairs and make 'em take out the dud ones, and label the ones in use with what they are. Can you get the Door Bells Mended, get the front porch floor cleaned and re polished. I'll keep sweating it out out here. Phone me a couple of times a week, more of ness.

Love to all (Le Barr included)

Spike

WED 3 Oct.

Dear Fat posh dolly bird,

Business. 1) Don't want to do The Commuter' its a Sellers cast off, I dont like secon hand clothes. Forget it.

2) If Phillip has nothing to do. Will he put all Press cuttings in order in my Press Books in my Private Cupboard on Landing.

3) Have you Paid Jack Hobbs for the printing of my dads 4 Books. If not do so.

4) Do Mermaid have a break down of how the finances of the Theatre work ? Like what salaries, what profits in Resturant, in other words a complete picture of Mermaids financial structure.

5) OK about Mermaid re election.

6. BARRY Green EMI. I wash my hands of anything to do with the LP Cover, after they behaved so abominiably last time including loosing my design, Sod 'em.

7) If they (EMI) want photos of Goons tell them we are not a photoagency for the Goon Show, the BBC are , like wise try Secombe and Sellers who do buggerall to put these records out, and collect money for it. No Photos tell them, all gone.

8 Gold Frame for my painting of coloured church windows, for Hattie Jaques. N.B. Make sure they Insure the paintings, each one is worth £ 150.

9+) When When When, is D Dobson printing the Bed Sit ? Hes had it over a year, and I keep getting letters about where people can get it. Will he please put it on the production line. Tell him this One year to get out a book is a bit slow by other firms standards,

10 Have BBC Sent Beachcomber Film yet URGENT. I must know while Im out here. So I can do something to make them get a move on. FLASH. I've jsut phoned Davic Stone of ABC out here, he has asked them for it, and it as yet has'nt arrived, will you ask them wahts the hold up ? PLEASE, GET SOME SENSE FROM THEM. Tell BBC I'm hanging on out here to see the print they send to view it with the ABC?.

11 Milliganimals, did you say its out in October ? Well if it is as Dobson to send me a copy, I could plug it out here,. In a rush to Post this

Phone me Love Spike

Dear Norma + Tams –

Not much time – hectic – one nighters – sleep in suit case – Did great at Twin Towns – Sell out at Wyella – Sell out Adelaide (1,500) Sold out at Renmark (to-night) sold out at Adelaide tomorrow (1,500) – But no life as such travel – perform – – Sleep – but its Barnstorming – Show Biz – going great – very hard to phone you as I write – its 11.20 am here but 10 to 3 in the morning UK – I leave here at 3 in afternoon – arrive Renmark 6 – ~~no~~ phone possible as its 9 am – I'm on at 7.30 – 11.30 your time

9 Orme Court,
LONDON. W. 2.

28th January, 1969

The Caxton Nameplate Co. Limited,
Kew Green,
Kew,
SURREY.

Dear Sirs,

I wonder if you could make for me, three small brass plates, with the following inscriptions.

1) This door was taken from 54 Hunter Street, London. the childhood home of J. Ruskin.

2) This fireplace was saved from 54 Hunter Street, London. the childhood home of J. Ruskin.

3) This console and mirror was taken from Brent Lodge, Finchley, before destruction by a Philistine Local Council.

The size should be 5" long by 2" wide, with screw holes at each of the four corners.

Perhaps you could let me know, as soon as possible, if you can do this for me.

Sincerely,

Spike Milligan.

The preservation Milligan. They were given to Bernard Miles for the Mermaid Theatre Museum.

Wildlife

9 Orme Court,
LONDON. W. 2.

Tel. PAR 2768

18th March, 1968

Peter Scott Esq.,
Wildfowl Trust,
Slimbridge,
GLOUCESTER.

Dear Peter,

I am writing to you about the condition, during the mating season of Mallards in Hyde Park, Kensington Park and St. James's Park.

The females are taking a terrible thrashing to the point of death which I have seen myself.

Having made a quick tour round the parks on Sunday the females are outnumbered 10-1, 5-1, and 3-1. Something has to be done.

The solution is very simple, to save gross maltreatment of the females, the males have got to be thinned out by shooting. The second, which would be much more difficult, would be trapping them at night by hand, taking them to distant parts of the country and releasing them which, of course, is out of the questi question.

The doddering Ministry of Public Buildings and Works, who should really be solving the problem are doing what most of the English are doing these days, flapping their hands and saying 'we can't do anything'.

So I am writing to you to ask for your help. I am writing around to other organisations, the R.S.P.C.A. my local M.P. and R.S.P.B.

The killings need not be useless, the ducks could be given to the Chelsea Pensioners who I am sure would enjoy eating them.

Do you know any good Wildfowlers who could shoot these, and are willing to come to London in the early hours of the morning before the parks are opened, and start thinning the males out.

Tons of love, keep fighting.

Spike Milligan

Conservationist.

9 Orme Court,
London, W.2.

13th March 1973

The Editor,
U.A.C.T.A. Magazine,
52 High Street,
Fordingbridge,
Hants.

Dear Vigilantes,

Just a line to ask you to bear in mind the precarious state of the whale. As you know, there has been no complete ban on whaling and some countries are still taking the most terrible toll of this magnificent and irresistible leviathan of the deep. I notice on page 4 of the current magazine that we are appealing for people to take specially printed postcards which can be forwarded to the Secretary of State and/or their Member of Parliament. I think whole schools ought to take them and send them en masse to our gentlement in parliament.

I want to thank you again for the efforts you are making, also to congratulate Joey Gregg and Trudi Harrison for winning the Dr. Albert Schweitzer Award. It makes me feel very good to know that young people are showing the way to a world of almost blind adults.

Love, Light and Peace,

Spike Milligan

9, Orme Court,
LONDON, W. 2.

1st June 1971.

The Lady who answers the 'phone
at 580-4034
Animals' Vigilantes,
51, Harley Street,
London, W1N 1DD

Dear Madam,

I am the impossible person who actually dared to ask you your name the other day. I find it almost unbelieveable to think that your parents took the loving care to baptize you as a child and you ignore that because you have become over bureaucrasized. The world that George Orwell predicted was opened up to me when you said the immortal lines "I am only allowed to give names of people of those in authority".

Supposing I would not give my name, how would we ever communicate? Cogitate on that dear nameless lady.

Sincerely,

Spike Milligan.

Compassion for the animals – but none for the 'nameless lady'.

With the approach of Christmas, the year 1975 draws to ~~and~~ a close - in retrospect was it a better world for animals? I'd love to say yes, but the answer is no. The horrible use of Beagles by ICI was one reminder of the debased levels at which our laughingly called 'civilization' works at. as I write this I read of more awful experiments at Cambridge University using kittens, the Import of animals by air continues, with absolutely no gorantee of their safety either by the Air-lines, the dealers or our own dear minister of..... Fred Peart, this month 2,000 little birds were delivered dead at London Airport - and what is degradingly immoral is, the Air Lines won't reveal the names of the dealers; I won't depress you further with these ~~acts of~~ monsterous acts by man, it's just to remind you that the need to fight ~~this~~ animal cruelty is even more important than ever, even when a law IS put forward ie The anti hare coursing Bill'

it fails to get thru ~~[illegible]~~ Parliament! And thats
the heart of our democratic life style -
remember, there are Members of Parliament
who are <u>MONSTERS</u>, when time comes to
vote ask them their views on Bloodsports
- etc, and vote accordingly. Now, happier
things, I want all children and their families
to have a <u>HAPPY</u> one, it doesn't have to be
an expensive one - just one with love
in the family - and love for nature and
humanity. I put nature first, because
without it there would be no mankind,
Think of the words of that very nice
man Jesus, all he preached was love
and truth towards all, if only those words
would get thru to the Fox Hunters -
the Veal Calf breeders - the Vivisectionists -
those awful men who take baby monkeys
away from their mothers just to see
what happens - we can only hope and
pray that one day .... I will spend
my Christmas with my family - and after
our Christmas Dinner - we will drink
a toast to all of you from us,

Love Light and Peace
from Spike

With the approach of Christmas, the year 1975 draws to a close in retrospect was it a better world for animals? I'd love to say yes, but the answer is no. The horrible use of Beagles by I.C.I. was one reminder of the debased levels at which our laughingly called "civilisation" works at, as I write this I read of more awful experiments at Cambridge University using kittens, the import of animals by air continues, with absolutely <u>no</u> guarantee of their safety either by the Airlines, the dealers or our own Minister of Agriculture, Fisheries and Food, Fred Peart, this month 2,000 little birds were delivered dead at London Airport - and what is degradingly immoral is, the Airlines won't reveal the names of the dealers; I won't depress you further with these monstrous acts by man, it's just to remind you that the need to fight animal cruelty is even more important than ever, even when a law is put forward, i.e. The Anti Hare Coursing Bill, it fails to get through Parliament. And, that's the heart of our democratic life style - remember, there are Members of Parliament who are <u>MONSTERS</u>, when time comes to vote, ask them their views on Bloodsports, etc. and vote accordingly.

Now, happier things, I want all children and their families to have a <u>HAPPY</u> one, it doesn't have to be an expensive one - just one with love in the family - and love for nature and humanity. I put nature first, because without it, there would be no mankind.

/Contd...

Think of the words of that very nice man Jesus, all he preached was love and truth towards all, if only those words would get through to the Foxhunters - the Veal Calf breeders - the Vivisectionists - those awful men who take baby monkies away from their mothers, just to see what happens - we can only hope and pray that one day ....
I will spend my Christmas with my family, and after our Christmas dinner - we will drink a toast to all of you from us.

Love, light and peace,

9 Orme Court
LONDON W2

20 November 1978

Animals' Vigilantes
James Mason House
24 Salisbury Street
Fordingbridge SP6 1AF

Dear Friends

I thought I would drop a message of Christmas good cheer to you all and try and encourage you in our unending fight for the world of animals.
I am sure you must have noticed the very very gradual change that is taking place in the attitue towards animals among those people at the top that are normally indifferent to animal suffering. The case in question was the success of animal lovers preventing the slaughter of 5,000 seals, as you know the number was reduced to 2,000. Even that is horrible but at least 3,000 seals are alive today because of people like ourselves, so we should feel well pleased that our efforts are showing some small measures of reward around the world.
Of course we must not let up for one moment because waiting to rush in at the least weakness are those people who thrive on using animals for profit. Even as I write you know full well that veal calves are being kept in little pens, battery hens in cooped up circumstances, all of which are totally abnormal and unnecessary, but apropro these creatures that none of our members should ever eat veal or take eggs from battery hens. Of course I am sure that none of you do.

.../

Anyhow Christmas is coming and I want you all to have as good a time as possible and remember that on that far distant Christmas when the Saviour was born he chose to have around him a cow, a donkey and a sheep. I think somehow there is a message in that.
A Very Merry Christmas to you all and keep fighting.

Love, Light and Peace

Spike Milligan

9 Orme Court,
LONDON. W. 2.

21st September, 1976

The Editor,
Daily Mail,
Fleet Street,
LONDON. E.C.4.

Sir,

Re Mr. Whiteley's quote "there must be an end to immigration", If he is saying they are worried about the number of immigrants, then is worry has come too late in the day to curb any increase.

I mean they are now procreating their own species in this country, so they come in via the womb.

It's too late, it's much too late to do anything about England maintaining an English character. We now have to become a Multi-racial society, and put up with it, so any thought of curbing immigration is just an anachronism; it's too late they are already here.

I am not a racialist, I am only commenting on the absurdity of the lack of logic among some politicians.

Sincerely,

Spike Milligan.

This is the sort of thing that got Spike branded as a racist – which he definitely was not. He was concerned about the dangers of unfettered immigration changing the English character – in 1976!

9 Orme Court
LONDON W2

1 February 1978

The Editor
The Guardian
119 Farringdon Rd
LONDON EC1

Dear Sir

Regarding the current racial furor.
God knows, I am an apostle of freedom, freedom for all I say, but there does come a point when one becomes suspicious as to the possibilities that can occur in a democracy if immigration is allowed to go unchecked. A prime example is Fiji where the native Fijians are now outnumbered by Asians. Democractically this means that the Asians should really now hold political power in the country and I know from personal experience that the Fijians are violently against this. Is it this which possibly makes lots of the native English worried about the future of immigration? I think yes, but in no way can these people be called racialists.
I would like readers reactions to this.

Yours

Spike Milligan

P.S. No "you are a racial bastard" letters please

Twenty-eight years later: how perspicacious and far-sighted – still going unchecked.

9 Orme Court
LONDON W2

10 May 1978

The Editor
The Guardian
119 Farringdon Road
LONDON EC1

Dear Sir

When Maria Colwell was killed by her father there was a great investigation into the injustice of her death. Recommendations were made and the laws appertaining to child welfare "tightened up". Yet I read (the Guardian 9 May) in 1975 Richard Fraser was admitted to hospital with 30 burns caused by cigarettes. How then in God's name was the child still in the "care" of the same parents in 1978?
No matter what any indignant Doctor, Welfare Worker, Policeman, neighbours, etc say, somewhere there is a person, if not persons, whose reactions to the cigarette burnings must have been tantamount to inertia. How long must a system exist when it is possible for a child to be gradually tortured and finally killed over a period of YEARS? If there was something rotten in the State of Denmark then there is something putrid in the Welfare State of England.

Yours faithfully

Spike Milligan

In answer to his question, posed in 1978: yes, the system still exists, but is much worse.

Maria Cowell

Goodnight Maria,
They have just changed you
from one darkness to another

You left behind
the eternal promise of light,
of seedlings
left in cruel frosts.

When spring comes
how many will miss your flower?
if you had grown
in my garden
We could have won
prizes together.

Goodbye Maria

Your gardners
are still alive

In a Taxi to some
pointless place
March '75

A poem he wrote for Maria Colwell.

Spike gave me this photo. 'Shame I didn't have his mind.' 'Einstein, I presume,' I said.

9 Orme Court,
LONDON. W. 2.

27th February, 1978

The Editor,
Guardian,
119 Farringdon Road,
LONDON. EC1R. 3ER.

Sir,

Reference the sex debate on Donald Duck. Fabian Acker suggests that there is no visible evidence of Donald Duck's male potential. May I point out to Mr. Acker that male ducks "don't let it all hang out". When needs be Donald most certainly could consummate the marriage with Daisy - Up-sa-daisey.

Sincerely,

Spike Milligan.

This was the Milligan I loved.

Dear Sir,

How long do we have to suffer authors who seek fame by ~~reversing history~~. ~~Sensationalism~~ sensationalism?. 'Lawrence made up rape story' (Sun Times. 12 June) Why stop there why not go the whole absurd hog, ie There was no such person as T E Lawrence - it was in fact D.H Lawrence in disguise - ~~who in fact~~. when T E Lawrence was supposed to be in Derra, it was not him, because ~~I can't prove~~ he was in fact playing second violin in Mrs Cruels Gipsy Trio at the ~~Fonton~~ Fontana Tea Rooms in Brighton. Likewise he never wrote the Seven Pillars of Wisdom, ~~he only wrote~~ that was his Aunt, [illegible] ~~Sandy~~ (Theyma) Edith Lawrence, a lesbian History teacher at ~~Red~~ Rhodean.. The man claiming to be Aircraftsman Shaw was in fact Capt Ball V.C. A believed ~~killed~~ shot down over France; who rejoined to avoid paying for his damaged aircraft. [illegible] ~~in fact he crashed lost his memory and was told he was Shaw by an Army Psychiatrist, was who an RAF recruiting depot. lost his memory,~~ The man killed on a motorbike was also not Lawrence - no, it was Tom Mountain a failed ~~impressionist~~ mime artist, disguised himself as Lawrence hoping to get some publicity - he did - in the Obituary Columns. The real T E Lawrence went on to change his name to Lee Harvey Oswald, the rest is history - except that the man who killed him was not Jack Ruby - it was Ronald Biggs who did the million pound train robbery to try and bribe Lord Goodman to defend him, to-day the Ronald Biggs in South America is only a plant, the real DH Lawrence to-day lives in retirement in Ditchling and collects ~~the~~ snails eggs, .

Sincerely –

Spike Milligan

I forgot! Wow!

PS Oh yes! Hitler by David Irving! Of course ~~but~~ Hitler didnt kill 6,000,000 Jews, impossible, because Hitler in fact was a life sized wooden dummy ~~(made from wood chopped by the Kaiser)~~ made by Nancy Mitford as a present for Martin Bormann, who used the dummy to blame for his own perverse sado-sexual desires. Ie: killing naked Jews? Who then committed suicide in the Bunker? It was a woman transvestite impressionist, Maria Schmells, who was standing in for the dummy while it was being treated for dry-rot, she was playing Irish Roulette (same as Russian only ~~all the chambers are~~ theres a bullet in every chamber) with Eva Braun, when an accident occurs..

SM

~~Why is P-E File?~~ ~~Then his letter to newspaper~~

~~Peregrine~~

9 Orme Court,
LONDON. W. 2.

13th June, 1977

~~Refused~~ Letter to newspaper

The Editor,
The Sunday Times,
200 Grays Inn Road,
LONDON. W.C.1.

Dear Sir,

How long do we have to suffer authors who seek fame by sensationalism? Lawrence made up rape story (Sunday Times 12th June), why stop there, why not go the whole absurd hog, i.e. there was no such person as T.E. Lawrence - it was, in fact, D.H. Lawrence in digguise - when T.E. Lawrence was <u>supposed</u> to be in Derra, it was not him, because he was, in fact, playing second violin in Mrs. Cruels Gipsey Trio at the Fontana Tea Rooms in Brighton. Likewise, he never wrote the Seven Pillars of Wisdom, that was his Aunt, Theresa Edith Lawrence, a Lesbian History Teacher at Roedean. The man claiming to be Aircraftsman Shaw was, in fact, Capt. Ball, V.C., believed shot down over France, who rejoined to avoid paying for his damaged aircraft. The man killed on a motorbike was also not Lawrence - no, it was Tom Mountain a failed mime artist, disguised himself as Lawrence, hoping to get some publicity - he did - in the Obituary Columns.

The real T.E. Lawrence went on to change his name to Lee Harvey Oswald, the rest is history - except that the man who killed him was not Jack Ruby - it was Ronald Biggs who did the million pound train robbery to try and bribe Lord Goodman to defend him, today the Ronald Biggs in

/Contd..

What would he have said about *The Da Vinci Code*?

South America is only a plant, the real D.H. Lawrence today lives in retirement in Ditchling and collects snails eggs.

Sincerely,

Spike Milligan.

P.S. Oh yes! I forgot - Wow! Hitler by David Irving! Of course, Hitler didn't kill 6,000,000 Jews, impossible, because Hitler, in fact, was a life sized wooden dummy made by Nancy Mitford as a present for Martin Bormann, who used the dummy to blame for his own perverse sado-sexual desires, i.e. killing naked Jews. Who then committed suicide in the Bunker? It was a woman transvestite impressionist, Maria Schmells, who was standing in for the dummy while it was being treated for dry rot, she was playing Irish Roulette (same as Russian only there's a bullett in every chamber) with Eva Bruan, when an accident occurs.

S.M.

/03

9 Orme Court,
LONDON. W. 2.

6th October, 1980

Lord Miles,
Mermaid Theatre,
Puddle Dock,
Blackfriars,
LONDON. E.C.4.

I am sorry I will be cruising somewhere in the Balearics on that day, but give my love to those swines who are making money by sitting at the telephone letting other people squander theirs. Tell them that I hope during the proceedings, Jesus does not repeat his entry, and do what he did to the money lenders.
I wonder what Ladbrokes were quoting when Jesus was on the Cross - "Would he go at 2-00 p.m. 3-00 p.m. or 4-00 p.m." or would the thieves each side of him (who were 100 to 1 on) become the favourites.
The golden sand of time is running, and I haven't seen you for nearly two years. Yet we love each other; why then is this pernicious system in charge of us, and not the reverse?
My love to Lady Miles.

Love, light and peace,

Spike Milligan.

P.S. I notice that your name hasn't gone metric yet.

A letter to a friend. 'The men in suits are trying to get rid of him', Spike prophesied. And they did.

SAME LETTER SENT TO:

FINANCIAL TIMES.
THE STAGE.

9 Orme Court,
LONDON. W. 2.

15th January, 1982

The Editor,
The Times,
200 Grays Inn Road,
LONDON. WC1. X8. EZ.

Dear Sir,

Many people from the entertainment world will be depressed at the forced resignation (for forced it was) of Sir Lew Grade.
It was Lew and Leslie Grade's agency which helped hundreds of us during the post war variety years, but for them it would not have existed. They only left it when they realised television was the coming thing.
O.K. so "Raise the Titanic" lost a lot of money. I ask you what Company doesn't. What about British Leyland, at least Sir Lew never went cap in hand begging for money, it was always on a business basis. What other Chairman would you find at his desk at 6-00 and 7-00 in the morning? Of course, he gave a large golden handshake, he was a big man, he still is a big man.
Holmes A'Court has got the Company, not because he is interested in show business, but because he is nothing more than a business magnate.
I am appalled at the short memories of the world of finance.
This man could have made it again and again if he was just given breathing space.

Sincerely,

Spike Milligan.

Defending a friend.

136

9 Orme Court,
LONDON. W. 2.

30th March, 1982

Lord Carrington, KC., MG., MC.,
Secretary of State for the
Foreign & Commonwealth Office,
King Charles Street,
LONDON. S.W.1.

Dear Lord Carrington,

Just to congratulate you and your Foreign Office on it's 200th Anniversary.
Thought you would like one from a clown.

Love, light and peace,

Spike Milligan.

He liked Lord Carrington and it shows.

9 Orme Court,
LONDON. W. 2.

12th March, 1984

Paul Getty Jnr. Esq.,
Tudor House,
16 Cheyne Walk,
LONDON. S.W.3.

My dear Paul,

Your kindness baffles me; we live in a society of human beings whose indifference can only be likened to a stagnant mill pond, where there is no sign of life above or below the water.

First of all these gifts of wine; I have a deep suspicion that you are trying to wean me on to high class expensive wines, so when I am finally hooked and incapable of buying these quality clarets, and I am trying to get a fix on cheap Sainsbury's Vin de Table (by then I might not even have a table) then, of course, I will have to come grovelling to you, my fixer, saying (in a Brooklyn accent) "give us a break, I've gotta have the money for another fix of Chateau Latour 1947". Of course, by then I will be totally within your power.

In return I am going to send you some flowers, I want you to get hooked on cheap hybrid freesia so that one day <u>YOU</u> will start grovelling to me saying "Spike freesia, I've got to have freesia, give us a break will you" So, even now the battle to the death is one, as to who gets hooked on what first.

I will come up and pay you a visit one evening, you will recognise me, I will be the one with the hyperdermic full

/Contd..

Paul Getty Junior loved receiving letters from Spike. He'd write to Spike just to receive a reply.

of Chateau Latour, which I will be mainlining into my throat.
I have just been reading Gershwins Years by Edward Jablonski and it gives an amazing feeling of the virility of America between 1918 - 1937. I could not help feeling that the opportunities presented to George and Ira Gershwin could not exist today, and I am trying to figure out why.
I have got a great idea, why don't we lease your father's Pompeian Villa at Malibu to McDonald's, and we could quote "Genuine Pompeian Big Mac and Chips, by Pliny the Younger", and how about McDonalds Pompeian Volcanic Holocaust Special, and finally, when are you going to admit that you really are Howard Hughes.

Love, light and peace,

Spike Milligan.

P.S. Try and get a cassette of Gershwin's Piano Concerto in 'F', which really represented America's break out into the classical world.

9 Orme Court,
LONDON. W. 2.

23rd March, 1984

Paul Getty Jnr.,
Son of Famous Piano Carrying Father,
Tudor House,
16 Cheyne Walk,
LONDON. S.W.3.

My dear Paul,

Seeing that you knew what it was like to have shit thrown at you from a crowd of Gooks, I am sending you a copy of books of war poems.
I belong to this Trust, and it is basically an attempt to get collections of poetry from soldiers, from ordinary G.I'S, up to Generals, some good some bloody awful.
Nevertheless, it's an insight into the state of men's minds under duress.
Amongst this batch you will find one of my own brilliant, super poems which makes Siegfried Sassoon fifty times better.
Anyhow, thought you might be interested.

Love, light and peace,

Spike Milligan.

9 Orme Court,
LONDON. W. 2.

6th December, 1983

George Harrison Esq.,
26 Cadogan Square,
LONDON. SW1X. OJP.

Dear George,

You once said to me - the world is full of arseholes, and I'm not one of them. I have a love for certain people and I have one for you, but by sheer lack of contact it's running out. I phone you frequently and never get a reply. This is what you do, it's very simple; you stand in front of a telephone and you insert your fingers in the holes and carry out a series of numbers which have been given to you. Of course, if you are rich you have buttons, which Irishmen usually sew on their coats.
Of course, if you are extremely rich you don't have to get in touch with anybody, and that's what I am worried about. The funeral takes place at Golders Green Crematorium, no flowers please, just money. You will recognise me, I am the dead one.

Love, light and peace,

Spike Milligan.

P.S. Thank you for sending the letter about the

/Contd..

Fender Guitar, believe it or not, I'm now playing the Guitar, and the silly bastards who insure it want living proof that it was a George Harrison Guitar, and I said to them, it was a George Harrison Guitar, but it is now mine.

9 Orme Court,
LONDON. W. 2.

12th January, 1984

Mr. & Mrs. P. McCartney,
MPL Communications Limited,
1 Soho Square,
LONDON. W.1.

Dear Paul & Linda,

Briefly, this is about the World you live in. As you know Greenpeace were responsible for finding the high radiation level off the coast near Windscale. They found it out for the human race, they did it for free, because of it, as you know the Government have closed the beach down.
For their trouble they are now going to be fined £50,000 in the Law Courts, and to pay this they are offering 64 shares, at £1,000 each in the vessel Cedarlea. I have bought one, would you like to, for the sake of the human race.
Do let me know.

Love, light and peace,

Spike Milligan.

Out with the begging bowl for the Beatles.

1 Soho Square · London W1V 6BQ · Telephone 01-439 6621 · Telex 21294

26th January 1984

Spike Milligan
9 Orme Court
London W2.

Dear Spike,

It is good to have people like you in the world.

Not only would we like one share of the Greenpeace boat at £1,000, but we would like one each - so that's two please!

Do let us have full details as soon as you can.

love,

Paul & Linda McCartney

9 Orme Court,
LONDON. W. 2.

26th January, 1984

Mr. & Mrs. Paul McCartney,
MPL Communications Ltd.,
1 Soho Square,
LONDON. W1V. 6BQ.

My dear Paul and Linda,

In this lonely fight people like you are a light in the darkness.
I tell you I have written to millionaires, and only two boys in the 'Pop' world, Elton John and yourselves have offered money.
Remember it's for your kids sake, and I don't know of a better investment, do you?

Love, light and peace,

Spike Milligan.

P.S. I am sending Linda a pound, to help pay the fine.

9 Orme Court,
LONDON. W. 2.

5th December, 1983

David Waddington Q.C., M.P.,
Minister of State,
Home Office,
50 Queen Anne's Gate,
LONDON. S.W.1.

Dear Mr. Waddington,

I am a Citizen of Eire; I used to be British but I lost my citizenship, after fighting seven years in the British Army, because somebody passed a Bill, and any son born of an Irish father, who was born before a certain date in Ireland was made Stateless.
As I have married a British wife, can I claim British citizenship now?

Sincerely,

Spike Milligan.

SM/NF

He was determined to keep up the pressure about his citizenship.

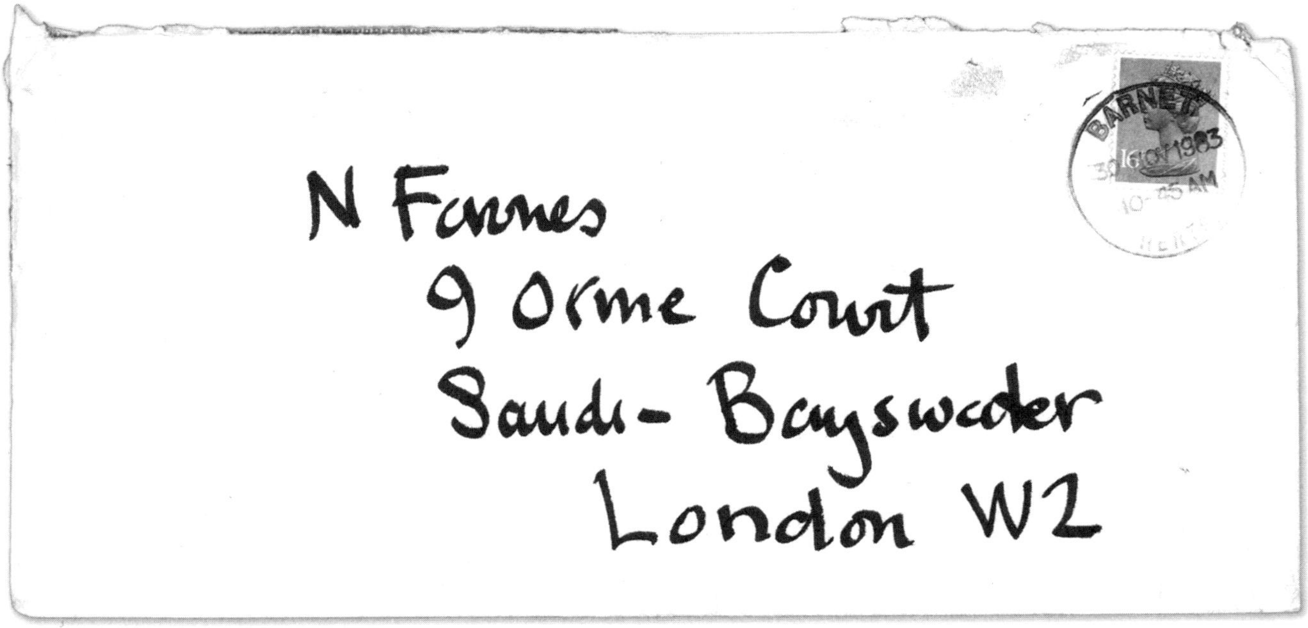

1983. He saw it coming.

(9)

9 Orme Court,
LONDON. W. 2.

1st August, 1983

Nick Curnow Esq.,
Phillips,
65 George Street,
EDINBURGH.

Dear Nick,

This is to confirm our telephone conversation that I will bid £6,200 for 'IN THE MIRROR'.
My contact will be my Manager, Norma Farnes, the late Lady Calthorpe. Will you please contact her, she has Power of Attorney over everything in my life except the Execution Squad.

Sincerely,

Spike Milligan.

DONT SEND — GO.

I went to Edinburgh. He didn't get his painting. He was devastated.

AUSTRALIAN NEWSPAPERS. 8/12/83.

RUMOURS OF MY DEATH ARE BASED
UPON SIMPLE FACT. RECENT NIGHTS I
HAVE TAKEN TO SLEEPING IN A
6'00" DEEP GRAVE. I HAVE FOUND THIS
HAS GREATLY REDUCED MY OVERHEADS AND
TAXES, AND PEOPLE ARE NOW FEELING
GENUINELY SORRY FOR ME. EACH MORNING
ON RISING CRIES OF "TIS A MIRACLE"
GOES AROUND LONDON.
OTHERWISE APART FROM A YOUNG LADY
CALLED MURIEL BODY I AM QUITE WELL.

SPIKE MILLIGAN

Spike 8/12/83
AUSTRALIAN ASSOC' PRESS

An Australian newspaper reported his death.

The bubble reads: 'If my nose gets any bigger its going to take over.'

9 Orme Court,
LONDON. W. 2.

21st February, 1984

Cliff Morgan Esq.,
British Broadcasting Corporation,
Kensington House,
Richmond Way,
LONDON. W.14.

My dear Cliff,

You must be dead, prior to this letter I have been trying to get in touch with you through a Welsh medium.
Briefly, the football Dodos are still stuffing in football scores during rugby matches, although they have changed the style. It was appalling, they gave nine football results in the first half of the Ireland/England match, and yet during the five minute interval, when they could have put the entire half time football results on they did nothing. Really Cliff, this is plain bloody stupid, surely you are not running a bloody stupid organisation. They really are the bitter end, and in this case, living evidence of it, is as I have just explained.
Phone me and apologise for Wales beating Ireland, and (b) phone me and I will tell you that France were very lucky to get away with it. Wales has all the makings of a splendid team. There was a disarming moment when they were on the French line, during the last ten minutes, when a more mature team would have scored, but by God the Welgh fire is being

/Contd..

Spike's hero: Spike was, in his own words, such a 'rugger bugger'.

stoked up again. It must have raised the hopes of Wales to see that performance.
I suggest, like always, the Irish will not beat Scotland, against all the odds; so far my predictions have been right, it was France, Scotland, and then a scrabble for third place.

Yours, still mad about the game.

Spike Milligan.
Dictated over the telephone and signed in his absence.

9 Orme Court,
LONDON. W. 2.

21st March, 1984

G.A. Griffiths Esq.,
District Works Officer,
Department of the Environment,
Buckingham Palace,
LONDON. S.W.1.

Dear Mr. Griffiths,

re: STREET LANTERNS IN
CONSTITUTION HILL.

Many years ago I was instrumental in preventing the street lights in Constitution Hill being pulled down; primarily because I discovered they were, in fact, the last in London with circular lanterns, in whose light possibly five generations of Monarchs had driven.

Alas, they were then converted from gas into what I believe orange sodium lighting, which gave off a hideous glare, and the Department was then forced to have frosted glass put into the lanterns. Everybody thinks this was a colossal mistake, and I did write originally to the Department and I got back a wishy washy letter stating "the whole of the lighting system in London is going to be re-investigated", I didn't know quite what that meant, but the appalling orange sodium lighting remains in Constitution Hill.

Both Prince Philip, and just three weeks ago, Prince Charles said "can you please try and do something about this lighting".

Originally I had said that the best method of conversion

/Contd..

His preservation mode.

would have been the green sodium lighting (I think that's the term) which you find in Regent's Park, adjacent to the Nash Terraces; this gives the effect of the original gas lighting, and does not dazzle on coming drivers.
I am sending a copy of this letter to Prince Philip and Prince Charles, so if you receive a personal visit from them do not be mystified.
I wonder if you would consider this suggestion. I appreciate the difficulty of the financial costs, but as I pointed out, everybody is dis-satisfied with the effect of the lighting in Constitution Hill.
My warm regards.

Sincerely,

Spike Milligan.

9 Orme Court,
LONDON. W. 2.

3rd April, 1984

H.R.H. The Prince of Wales, K.G., K.T.,
Buckingham Palace,
LONDON. S.W.1.

Dear Prince Charles,

You will be getting a long bumpf letter from Mr. G.A. Griffiths, Department of the Environment, all I asked him was could he change the orange sodium lamps in Constitution Hill, to gas green sodium lamps.
He could have just said yes or no, he hasn't, just thought you would like to know.

Love, light and peace,

Spike Milligan.

Same letter to Prince Philip.

9 Orme Court,
LONDON. W. 2.

30th April, 1984

Michael Parkinson Esq.,
Lyndal Mount,
Fishery Road,
Bray,
BERKS.

Dear Michael,

I believe that you are taking over from poor Michael Aspel, how can you put this poor father of four out of work like this.

It's a coincidence that I have been asked to appear on this programme to help the ratings, it means, of course, that I will have to leave your poor mother in the work-house for that day.

She still asks about you and yours, and thanks you for the parcels of pile ointment.

Yours,

Nurse Milligan.

Amusing Michael Parkinson, or trying to.

9 Orme Court,
LONDON. W. 2.

10th April, 1984

The Editor,
Guardian,
119 Farringdon Road,
LONDON. E.C.1.

Dear Sir,

Help. My father was British, my grandfather was British, my mother is British, and my brother is British, I was British. I served seven years in the army during the last war.

In 1960 I went to renew my British Passport, and was told I was no longer entitled to it, and in the words of the chinless wonder at the counter I was "now Stateless". Some idiotic law had been passed, and they said I could re-apply. I was so incensed I didn't think a country that treated me like this deserved me, so I became a Citizen of Eire.

I have since tried to become a British Citizen again, but have always been given a mass of forms to fill in, and told to get in the queue. I found this appalling treatment, but now I see that if you can run a certain distance in world record time, and your father is British, you can get a passport within ten days. The jolly chap from the Home Office on television last night said "we do grant passports to people whose parents are British if they are particularly talented".

Without sounding egotistical, I thought I was a talented member of the society, having entertained it for some

/Contd..

He won't let go: he's now becoming an embarassment. He loved that.

30 years during which time I received the very first ever British Writer's Television Award, and yet I still remain a foreigner.

I wrote to the Home Secretary personally over a week ago, telling him they owed me a British Passport for my services to this Country, so far dead silence. If I don't receive a reply soon, you will see me training for the world mile record which will, no doubt, guarantee me a passport.

Sincerely,

Spike Milligan.

9 Orme Court,
LONDON. W. 2.

10th May, 1985

The Editor,
Daily Mirror,
Holborn Circus,
LONDON. E.C.1.

Sir,

It was very touching to see the letter written by your readers Brian and Pamela Dean regarding the way the Home Office refused my British Passport, and despite a letter to The Queen, Mrs. Thatcher and the Home Secretary I am still treated at arms length, and the only way to re-entry is to fill in forms and take an oath of allegiance to the Queen. I thought having risked my bloody life for five years in the last war was sufficient evidence to prove my loyalty.

I have not given up the fight, I am currently enquiring as to how Yehudi Menhuin was given a British Passport without having to go through the normal channels, as quoted in The Times.

All the flag waving and speech making on V.E. Day didn't mean a thing to me, I just felt I didn't belong to this anymore, and it is a very sad state of affairs to arrive at. Thank you Great Britain; no wonder the natives asked us to leave India. Mind you, half of them are now British Citizens - see you in Australia folks, they like me out there.

Sincerely,

Keep it up, Spike.

9 Orme Court,
LONDON. W. 2.

10th May, 1985

The Rt. Hon. Leon Brittan, Q.C., M.P.,
Secretary of State for the Home Office,
50 Queen Anne's Gate,
LONDON. S.W.1.

Dear Mr. Brittan,

I notice in The Times (3rd May) Yehudi Menhuin a Swiss National has been given British Nationality, and to quote him "did not have to make an official application to the Home Office, the details of which are confidential". Does this present a fresh opportunity for me to be granted British Citizenship without the necessity of going through the procedure, which as you know I find extraneous; having proved my loyalty to the Crown having served five years in the British Army, and apart from which being a member of 20 sterling British organisations, many of which I am Vice President like the British Trust for Conservation Volunteers - but no longer being British I ought to resign. I wonder if there is any new light in this stupid dark bureaucratic tunnel.

Yours sincerely,

Spike Milligan.

Now it's the Secretary of State's turn.

9 Orme Court,
LONDON. W. 2.

7th June, 1985

The Rt. Hon. Leon Brittan, Q.C., M.P.,
Secretary of State for the Home Office,
50 Queen Anne's Gate,
LONDON. SW1H. 9AT.

Dear Leon,

Thank you for your letter, you sound a decent enough chap. O.K. so the "Times" article was misleading (God save us from our misleading newspapers).
I was brought up on the principle of the Socratic argument, there can only be one truth, and that sometimes is outside of the law. I am still totally baffled as to having been born British, to British parents, living as a British person in England for most of my life, partly in India, serving the British Crown - one moment I am British and then at the stroke of a pen I am not British. You see I don't mind the law being an ass, but being a total bloody fool is another thing.
What galls me, dear Leon, is the fact that having risked my life in the service of the Crown and proved my loyalty in more than 100 ways, I find it galling that I should be put in the position of asking to take the Oath of Allegiance to the Queen; which can only mean up to that stage I have not been allegiant to the Queen, that can be the only process of that ceremony. It's rather like a constable seeing a man shoot a person dead and then arresting the corpse for being murdered. I find this allegiance to the Queen ceremony as demeaning, by that degree of logic.
In referring to the law that brought this ridiculous situation about, I cannot see what the vista was in creating this dispossession of a person's British nationality, I can't see any rationale in it at all, if it was an attempt to stop the flood gates of immigration, as you know this failed

/Contd..

miserably.
Once again on the Socratic argument of truth, it seems strange you yourself being Semitic by descent are the Home Secretary, whereas I who have Scottish, English and Irish blood, and therefore, much more British ethnically, am really not British. It's as Alice said "It's all very strange".
However, I know you are a kindly man and a gentleman and if you are very very good you might get invited to have dinner at my place - that is, I hope you do not mind dining with foreigners.
I give you my warm regards because of you personally bending over backwards for me to become British - but wait - another thought, if I have to pay £55 to get a British Passport why did they not give me £55 for it when they took it away from me?
My word, didn't we Australians give you Pommies a thrashing in the two one day cricket matches.

Love, light and peace,

Spike Milligan.

The pure logic of £55. And when did he become an Australian?

LORD BERNSTEIN, LL.D. *President*

GRANADA GROUP LIMITED

Granada Television
Granada T V Rental
Granada Theatres
Granada Publishing
Granada Motorway Services
Barranquilla Investments
Novello Music

36 Golden Square London W1R 4AH *Telephone: 01-734 8080 Telegrams: Granada London*

2nd July 1985

Dear Spike,

I have your 'exploratory' letter of 20th June and on the strength of that letter I have persuaded my TV Rental colleagues to give you the black and white portable Sony TV with their love and good wishes.

Mr David Parish, one of GTVR's top bosses, will turn this note into official bumpf any day.

It was good to hear from you.

As ever,

Sidney

Mr Spike Milligan,
9 Orme Court,
London W2

10/JM/PPL

20 June letter – lost. Spike wrote, 'I've rented my TV too long; it's about time you gave it to me.' Lord Bernstein's reply.

9 Orme Court,
London W 2.

17th July 1985.

The Lord Bernstein LLD,
Granada Group Ltd,
36 Golden Square,
London W1.

Dear Sidney,

Thank you for speaking up for Granada so bravely. Believe it or not my manager has just asked me to sign a petition to the Soviet Ambassador saying Anatoly Shcharansky should be allowed to join his wife Avital in Israel; so you can tell I am partially converted, which is how my last mini metro sounded when I was driving.
I must tell you that the letter was really sent in the spirit of a joke trying to break your day to day mundane inflow of mail.
Anyhow looking at the set this very minute, and I see to my horror it's gone on the blink, do you have exorcist powers??.

Love, light and peace.

Spike Milligan,

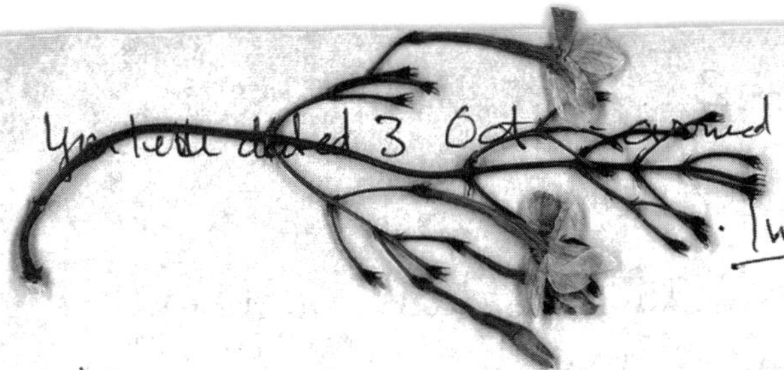

Yr letter dated 3 Oct arrived today 9 october. I'm replying at once

My dear Norma -

Business letter.

1) Phantom, Raspberry blower'. Keep it on ice till I get back. Peter Sellers once said he'd like to do it as a film. So I'll investigate that channel - as it would be more lucrative as a film..

2) Goon Record. In the Goons there are numerous occassions where either P. Sellers - or myself play a chord or our own tune on the piano, can they find one such occassion - and put that on the end. ~~in place of~~ I'm in no rush to get it on by christmas - I'd I want to get it right - they just want to rush it - in heapes of money. Believe me, no matter when they issue it - it will sell well - anytime. So let them stew.'

3) Duncan Woods - Beachcomber TV. I want to see the script - because Barry Took has never written anything on his own - he's always had a co writer - and I dont think he can write good stuff on his own.

4) D Sellinger - Film. Sounds O.K - . depends on Oblomov - (I dont think its going to happen) Film world is much more lucrative. Tell him (Dennis) to carry on as tho' Oblomov didn't exist. I'd like to see script.

Sending me a pressed flower. What did he want me to do that I know I wouldn't have wanted to do?

Julie Felix show

1) Is it a variety show with audience? If so, you can't go on and read childrens poetry - you have to do an act - with a proper ending

2) If its just a studio show - then I can do a more 'literary act' ie Reading from 'Puckoon' or the like.

3). How many minutes

4) Is there an Orchestra

5) OK I'll talk to Dorfman when I return

Jimmy Verner - 1) I am only doing this tour - because there was no other continuous work available -, 2) I have only agreed (not signed) to do Bradford - 3 Weeks in Dublin - and a promise to David Conyers to do Blackpool (as I had not done the ~~Blackpool the~~ Blackpool week they were expecting me to do) after that - nothing.

Losing Phantom Rasberry blow - is a bit of a financial shock - I was using that show to free me to Work over December - so I'll have to complete the Current Bed-Sit Tour. Bradford - Dublin - Blackpool - no agreed dates till I get back – and see what real work exists – because promises in this proffession, rarely become reality [Like the bird who gave me Champagne – and wanted me to make a film of London Buildings]

Now are there any Pantomimes going – ? ~~[illegible]~~
Ask Bernard Delfont – he likes me
Ones with limited 8 week runs like – Golders Green – ?
limited because of Oblomov –
1 This Oblomov is a bloody nuisance – its holding me back. – Can you phone Cindy Daggine – and ask her how near to a reality is Broadway? –
PS. If I was offered a Big Panto, long run; good money (like Palladium) – Then take it – Oblomov will have to wait.

I have a deal to put on Bed-Sit here in Sydney. – Tell you about it when I come back.

Needless to say BMC never ever phoned me to say 'No Car' – I waited 4 days – (Twit) then I did a TV – interview – in exchange they have given me a car free for the holiday. Tell the gentleman at BMC England Thanks for nothing – especially the indifference – good job I can read the future

4

I *knew* there would be no Car.

I promise 200 Cigarettes.

I'll let you know the flight etc.

Give Eric my regards - tell him lets get together when I return.

SUN! SUN! Sea - Beaches - Mountains Flowers - Women with Big

!! And

Wine! (Iced!)

As Ever
Spike

Excuse awful writing - but I'm on holiday

9 Orme Court
Bayswater
London W2 4RL

Rt Hon Tony Blair
Prime Minister
10 Downing Street
London
SW1A 2AA

July 24th 1997

Dear Tony,

Whilst you are doing so much for the human race would you spare a thought for those fur bearing animals. That's all.

LOve,light and peace,

SPIKE MILLIGAN

We agreed some time later. He thought about neither.

Spike Milligan

9 Orme Court
Bayswater
London
W2 4RL

Fax To: Daily Mail
Letters Page
Northcliffe House
2 Derry Street
London W8 5TT
0171-937-7493

August 5th 1998

Sir,

I was horrified that the Roman Catholic religion refused to bury Eva Bartok. The Message Jesus gave to Mary Magdalene was 'Go and sin no more' - an act of forgiveness which apparently the Roman Catholic church are bypassing.

Yours horrified catholic,

Spike

SPIKE MILLIGAN

Spike Milligan

Fax:0171-782-5046

9 Orme Court
Bayswater
London
W2 4RL

The Editor
The Times
News International
1 Virginia Street
London
E1 9BD

September 21st 1998

Sir,

What Foreign Office idiot sent the Queen to a riot infested country. One day they will get it right.

Sincerely,

Spike

SPIKE MILLIGAN

Nothing changes.

Dear Jack + Norma.

I'm a bit overwhelmed by magnificent and generous birthday present it was more than a present it was like a dowery. if I control myself it will last till my next birthday. the question is will I.

Love

Spike

I'm glad I got it out of the office before Jack spotted it!

In his later years his favourite wine was an Australian Burgundy, Grange Hermitage, which cost an arm and a leg. We bought him six bottles for his 75th birthday.

The End